Unexpected Admirer

By Bernadette Marie

This is a fictional work. The names, characters, incidents, places, and locations are solely the concepts and products of the author's imagination or are used to create a fictitious story and should not be construed as real.

5 PRINCE PUBLISHING AND BOOKS, LLC
PO Box 16507
Denver, CO 80216
www.5PrinceBooks.com

ISBN 13: 978-1-63112-025-1 ISBN 10: 1631120255
Unexpected Admirer
Bernadette Marie
Copyright Bernadette Marie 2013
Published by 5 Prince Publishing

Second Edition/Second Printing February 2014 Printed U.S.A.

5 PRINCE PUBLISHING AND BOOKS, LLC.

Unexpected Admirer

Aspen Creek Series, Book Two

Other books by
Bernadette Marie

THE KELLER FAMILY SERIES

ASPEN CREEK

MATCHMAKERS SERIES

OTHER TITLES

5 Prince Publishing, Denver Colorado

To Stan
You certainly were my unexpected admirer…good thing I caught on!

Acknowledgements

To my men…thank you for allowing me to lock myself away with imaginary people! My job is full of play time.

To Mom and Dad…thank you always for your love and support.

To Anni…thank you for always reading my stuff in all its forms. And for laughing when you're supposed to and crying at the right times as well.

To Connie…what a mess I'd be…just saying!

To Anne…thank goodness you came along!

To Susan…I'm glad you happened into my life and taught me everything you know!

And a special thank you to Justin Timberlake…your talent and good looks made it easy to imagine someone as sincere as Jesse Charles!

Dear Reader,

Thank you for stopping back into Aspen Creek for the next story in the series. This town is so much fun to write. There are so many stories hiding among the residence here.

The story of Melissa Mathews and Jesse Charles is a fun one. What happens when the rock star falls in love with the middle school biology teacher? Sometimes the bright lights of fame are a little to blinding. There are those times when the simple life is much more appealing.

While in Aspen Creek we run into some of the characters we met in the past, and those are the joys of reading a series.

I hope you enjoy Unexpected Admirer and I look forward to sharing the next book in the series with you in September. *On Thin Ice* is very near and dear to my heart. If you know me, you know that hockey is very important in my family and the next Aspen Creek book will take you on the ice.

As always…enjoy a little *Happily Ever After.*

Happy Reading,
Bernadette Marie

Unexpected Admirer

Chapter One

A crowded arena on a weeknight was not where Melissa Mathews wanted to be. She'd spent her day teaching thirteen-year-olds the fundamentals of biology, attended a staff meeting, and drove an hour to Grand Junction. She was beat.

But when she looked over at her son, who stood next to her, his grin as big as the sun, she knew she'd recuperate. After all, it was her fault they were standing with thousands of people who chanted Jesse Charles's name. She'd won the tickets to see the pop star on the radio. The show had been sold out for months, and she didn't have the funds to take her son anyway.

It was a mystery to her why he even wanted to go. Jonah was a huge Jesse Charles fan, but Melissa wasn't. Oh, he seemed to be a fine role model, but between her son playing his music morning and night and the kids at school incessantly talking about him, Melissa could care less about the man.

And the night was just beginning. No, she couldn't have just won some general admission tickets. She won the whole package. A nice dinner at a local restaurant. Front row tickets to the show. And what would a night like this be without meet and greet passes for later.

Jonah was in heaven.

Melissa was in a teenager-fueled hell.

Jesse Charles paced back and forth in his dressing room. He'd been performing since he was ten, professionally since he was fourteen. However, stage fright was a real thing and he had it bad.

His assistant, Bryce, was busy taking notes and talking on his cell phone in the corner. He'd thought his manager would take the time to fly to Colorado to catch the show, but again, he was busy with his own, fantastic life.

Jesse let out a sigh. His career was nothing less than spectacular. He was the number one recording artist in America, and the world had taken note.

But at twenty-five, Jesse Charles was tired.

Melissa fidgeted with the backstage pass around her neck. The woman at the radio station had told her to keep it under her shirt. She'd seen people mobbed over them. It was killing Melissa to have it pressed against her skin, but the last thing she needed was to have it ripped from her neck. Jonah hadn't been happy about tucking his in either, but he'd done it. What did it matter anyway? He was going to meet his idol. All Melissa could hope for was to be in bed before two a.m. and that maybe Friday would be quiet for the middle-schoolers she'd have to teach—but she knew better than that.

The lights in the arena dimmed, and the crowd around her went wild. She looked over at her son. An enormous smile permeated his lips. He hadn't been so happy in a very long time. Melissa owed him this night. She put her arm around him and gave him a squeeze just as the arena filled with lights of all colors. A whine of a guitar pierced her ears, and from the center of the stage in a smoke-filled cloud, Jesse Charles emerged in all his glory.

She had to admit, the atmosphere was infectious. Girls swooned and screamed. Jonah clapped his hands and sang along with the songs she was familiar with, but she didn't know the words. Never would she have expected to enjoy herself, but among Jesse Charles's fans, she was happy too.

The show was loud and spectacular—and never ending.

Melissa looked down at her watch for the third time. The show was moving into its second hour, and the man hadn't taken a break. He'd sung and danced the entire time—he had endless energy. She, on the other hand, was exhausted.

Melissa scanned the crowd. She was sure she was the only person aware of the time. She looked back up at the stage, and at that moment, she was sure her eyes connected with Jesse Charles's. The very moment hit her.

She diverted her eyes. Certainly he was that good of a showman to make the entire audience feel as though they were the only ones in the room.

It wouldn't be long before she'd be right in front of him, shaking his hand. But that was all for Jonah. She wasn't interested. She was sure he'd say hello, sign a picture, and move on to the next person. Yes, that would be how it would go. She told herself there really hadn't been any eye contact. Thousands of scantily clad girls screamed his name. If he had seen her, it was probably a look of disgust for someone so average in his crowd.

Jesse Charles went about belting out the song of the moment. He danced his way to the side of the stage, motioned to someone, and without missing a beat, he was back at center stage making the crowd go wild.

A few minutes later, Melissa felt a hand on her shoulder.

"Ma'am, would you mind coming with me?" An enormous man with a security shirt was standing next to her.

"I'm sorry," she yelled over the music. "Did I do something wrong?"

"If you wouldn't mind just coming with me."

He was trying to guide her away from her seat. "My son!"

She reached for Jonah and grabbed hold of his arm and then quickly picked up their coats.

As she followed the man, another security guard stepped in behind them. Jonah moved up closer to her.

"Where are we going?"

"I don't know." She reached out for the man in front of her as they headed toward the side of the arena. "Sir, where are we going?"

"I've been asked to take you backstage."

Melissa let out a breath. "Is this for the meet and greet?"

"No." The guard narrowed his gaze on her.

"Oh, we have passes." She pulled the pass from under her shirt.

"No, ma'am, this has nothing to do with that. Mr. Charles would like to sing to you. He's requested you on stage."

Certainly there was some kind of mistake. The radio station hadn't said anything about getting on stage.

Her heart pounded faster than the rhythm of the song blaring thought the arena.

Jonah had grabbed hold of her hand. "Mom! He wants to sing to you!"

"I don't like this."

The men were leading them down a corridor The music was muffled, but as they turned the corner, she could see the stage and Jesse Charles was only a few feet in front of them, performing for thousands.

"What if I don't want to do this?"

The security guard gave her a shrug.

Jonah stepped between them and looked up at her. "Mom, this is fun. Go."

When did a ten-year-old tell his mother what to do? But then she noticed the glimmer in his eyes and the smile that still turned his lips up at the corners. She couldn't let him down.

She handed Jonah her coat, straightened her clothes, and ran her fingers through the wild curls which went every which direction. This had to be some kind of a joke for the superstar. What a mother wouldn't do for the joy of her child.

Jesse glanced to the side of the stage. Bryce had made his way to the woman he'd pointed out in the crowd. He was obviously giving her directions, but even Bryce was probably thinking he was crazy.

Never, in all the years that he'd been performing, had he ever pulled someone from the crowd to sing to, but there was something about this woman that had caught his attention. Perhaps it was because she stood out simply by not standing out.

The blouse she wore was a simple, white button-down with a pair of jeans. Her hair was a wonderment of wayward, brown curls. But from the row in front of the stage, her eyes had sparkled up at him and caught hold.

The song ended, and the lights dimmed. His band carried on as the crew pulled two stools to the center of the stage.

Jesse let out a breath. Stage fright was bad enough, but walking toward this woman, he decided it was the lesser of two evils.

The eyes that had mesmerized him now were wide open, perhaps a bit fearful.

He smiled and tried to calm his own nerves. "Hi, I'm Jesse." He held his hand out to her.

"Melissa."

"It's nice to meet you." He kept hold of her hand. "I'd like to sing to you."

She nodded as though words were impossible. He understood that well enough. He hoped he remembered the song now that she stood before him.

Jesse switched hands and led her out to the stage where the crew member helped her onto her stool, but he never let go of her hand.

The music formed into the melody the world had accepted. His most current number one hit had given him the leap to super stardom and he hated it, but it encompassed what he was feeling at that very moment.

As the lights came up and he could see her face even more clearly, he knew this would be the hardest song he would ever sing. He, the man who dated super models and actresses, was nearly paralyzed by her beauty. There were no Botox-filled lines, no four-inch high heels on her feet, or even a trace of lipstick on her lips. If anyone he knew found out his heart was flipping in his chest over this woman, they'd have him committed.

Melissa's hand shook in his. He covered the mic on his cheek. "Are you okay?"

She nodded as the volume of the music increased, and the crowd around them erupted into applause.

Jesse took a breath and began to sing the ballad of *Admirer* to the woman who had him as giddy as a schoolboy.

Chapter Two

Melissa was afraid to look toward the audience. Dear Lord, why was she sitting on the stage holding hands with this young man? No one at the radio station had told her this was part of the show.

She did manage to look back at Jonah, who stood on the side of the stage with her purse grasped in his arms. The smile on his face was enormous and that made her happy, and she realized, in that moment, it had been a very long time since she'd been this happy, too.

Jesse's thumb brushed over her hand, and when she looked back in his eyes, they pulled her in. So this was what those girls who swooned over the posters in their lockers felt like? But she wasn't some thirteen-year-old-girl. She was a mother, a widow, a biology teacher. It wasn't right to feel warm from head to toe because Jesse Charles was gazing at her. She was probably old enough to be his mother. How sweet that he was singing to her. They probably all thought that when he pulled a strange woman onto the stage each night.

But Melissa couldn't deny that there was more, and she felt it. In two and a half minutes, she'd be just another fool slobbering over herself because of his smile. Even as he gave her hand a squeeze, she knew she had to be smart about what was stirring inside of her. She was thirty-five years old. And she'd been schooled in realism. Losing her husband when he'd performed a routine traffic stop was realistic. Raising her son, taking care of her mother, and making a living as a teacher in a very small town was the reality of her life. Sitting with Jesse Charles was just a moment, literally in the spot light, which she'd look back on and smile.

At the end of the song Jesse stopped singing. But the song continued on, and the words were loud in her ears. It was as if they pulled her from the trace that his eyes had put her under, and she looked out to see the glow of lighters and cell phones waving in a sea of people who finished the song.

Her body trembled.

Jesse lifted his hand to her cheek and guided her attention back to him as he sang the very last line.

The crowd erupted into applause, and Jesse Charles moved in closer to her and kissed her.

The whole world must have stopped in that moment because all she could hear was her heartbeat in her ears.

When the kiss ended and she looked into the eyes of Jesse Charles, she wondered why he looked so shaken. Surely kissing another woman each night made him immune to anything. Was it so bad, her kiss?

She watched him suck in a deep breath and then cover the mic on his cheek as the lights dimmed. "Wow. I hope you didn't mind that."

"It was nice of you."

His expression changed as if she'd offended him.

"I've never done that before. There was something about you…"

A stagehand was standing next to her ready to push her offstage and back to the side where she'd come from. She jumped off the stool and turned toward Jonah, who was still grinning.

Jesse grabbed her hand. "Wait. Don't let them make you leave."

Melissa narrowed her stare. "I have backstage passes for me and…"

"Good!" His eyes widened as the music grew louder. "I'll see you soon."

The crew member guided her off to the side of the stage, and Jesse went about his work mesmerizing the crowd.

"Mom! Mom! He kissed you!" Jonah dropped her purse on the ground and enveloped her into an enormous hug. "Did you see that?"

She wondered if he knew how silly it sounded. "Yes, I was there."

Bryce, the man with a striking resemblance to Jesse Charles who had earlier introduced himself as Jesse Charles's assistant, walked over to them. "Mr. Charles has requested that you both watch the show from here."

"I didn't realize the meet and greet passes included all of this." Melissa looked down at her pass dangling around her neck.

"It doesn't. He seems to be out of sorts this evening. He's never been one to pull women on stage. He thinks it's tacky."

Jesse was doing his job, hitting the notes, giving the audience what they'd paid their hard-earned money to see, but his eyes were on the side of the stage.

Melissa had been shoved off, beyond the audience's view, and now was embraced by a young boy. Why had he thought she'd be another one of the single women in the crowd? She had a son, which more than likely meant she had a husband.

Well, he'd play it off as a moment to sing to a fan. No one would be the wiser, but he'd feel like the fool. He'd probably have one pissed of man after him, too.

Just one more song, and he'd go make nice with the son. Salvage the night, and maybe she wouldn't think he was such an idiot.

After he'd sung his final song he hurried offstage, and Bryce met him, as always, with a towel and a bottle of water.

"Another great show."

Jesse sucked down the water. "The altitude is torture."

"I just think you're a wimp."

Jesse laughed as he finished off the bottle of water. "What did you do with Melissa?"

The smirk on Bryce's face was all the razzing he'd get over asking some woman on stage. Jesse knew that.

"She's over in the corner with her son. You've never done that before," he said as they walked toward them, Bryce keeping close to him—as though to protect him as he always did.

Knowing Bryce was his closest confidant, he could be honest. "There was something about her. I needed to see her."

"She's not your type."

"And I have a type?"

Bryce chuckled. "Well, let's say she's not the type Carson gives you."

"He can bite me. That last woman he put me with, the model, I'm sure she didn't have an ounce of intelligence in her head."

"Well, honey, I could have told you that." Bryce patted him on the back before he turned his head and gave a very blatant look at the ass of one of the stagehands. "Is he taken?"

Jesse laughed as they made their way to Melissa, who was busy looking down at the young boy who he could only hear was speaking much too fast.

"Hi." His voice shook as he approached them. The boy stopped talking and turned to look up at him. It was most definitely her son. He had the same eyes which had caught Jesse off guard.

Melissa placed her hands on the boy's shoulders. "Jonah, this is Mr. Charles. Can you say hello?"

"Hi," the boy's voice squeaked, and Jesse decided they were in the same boat. He was as shaken meeting Jesse as Jesse was having met Melissa.

Jesse held out his hand. "What's your name?"

"Jonah."

"Jonah, it's nice to meet you. Thanks for letting me borrow your mom."

"Oh, sure."

Melissa kept her hand on his shoulder—and her gaze, too. Jesse's own mother had never looked at him like that. Who would have thought he could be jealous over such an endearing moment.

There was a tightening in his chest, and he didn't like it. Even if the woman was someone else's wife, he could salvage the time. Jonah looked like the kind of kid who needed a special moment. Even though his mother looked down at him with pure love in her eyes, there was sadness in his.

Jesse reached for Jonah's pass, which hung around his neck. "I see that you were coming back here to see me anyway."

"Mom won the tickets on the radio."

Jesse shifted his glance from the boy to his mother. There was a blush to her cheeks. The ache in his chest deepened. He didn't need to hear much more, he knew she was a special woman.

He looked back at Jonah. "What does your dad think of you two staying out so late?"

Jesse smiled and looked at Melissa, but the smile that had permeated her lips since he'd met her backstage slipped away and Jonah's head lowered. He'd said something horribly wrong.

"Jonah's father died three years ago." Melissa's voice had softened, but her hand remained on his shoulder.

"I'm sorry." Jesse swallowed hard. "My dad died when I was ten. It was hard."

Jonah looked up at him. His eyes had grown damp. "I miss him."

They had a connection—him and this young man.

Bryce caught Jesse's attention. The show might be over, but the stage fright was still very real. It was time for the doors to open and the fans that adored him to come in a gawk. He was thankful for them all, but he didn't enjoy the closeness. Perhaps he'd learned that from his mother. She'd kept her distance his whole life, staying only close enough to dive into his wealth when she needed.

Jesse sucked in a breath.

"Jonah, would you like to meet all these people with me?"

Jonah's head lifted, and he looked back at his mother. "Can I?"

"Oh, you should stay out of Mr. Charles's…"

"Jesse," he corrected her.

Melissa looked up at him and smiled before she looked back at Jonah. "You should stay out of Jesse's way."

"Really, he wouldn't be in the way." He leaned in closer to her. "I'd enjoy the distraction."

Jonah looked up at his mother again. "Please."

Melissa dropped her shoulders. "For a little bit. We need to get home. We have school tomorrow."

Jesse found humor in that. "You go to school?"

Melissa narrowed her brows and then the smile was back as she understood what he'd said. "I'm a teacher. Middle school biology."

"You're much too pretty to be a biology teacher."

Her cheeks filled with color. "Well, thank you. I'm sure my students figure I fit the part."

He didn't suppose she knew what they really thought. The woman was making his head spin and he'd been with women that society deemed perfect. They hadn't cut it, but she...

Bryce nudged him. "They're ready to open the door."

"Jonah is going to be my assistant tonight."

Bryce nodded. "Oh, good. My replacement. C'mon, Jonah, I'll show you what we need to do."

Melissa watched her usually shy son walk away with the man who obviously spent his life taking care of the pop star.

"Really, you don't have to do this."

"He's a great kid. Is he ten?"

"Yes. It's been a long time since I've seen him smile as much as he did tonight. Thank you for that."

Jesse ran his hand over his hair. "That is certainly validation for my job."

"Well, a mother can't give a son who has lost so much that kind of joy."

"I think you're selling yourself short."

Why did this man find it necessary to flatter her? She was nothing to him, but his charm on her was working.

Jesse looked toward the door where a crowd stood just beyond a large man who held them out. "I suppose I'd better get over there. I'll keep an eye on him."

"Thank you."

He touched her arm as he passed by her, and a shiver ran through her. What was it about this young man that had her mind turning to mush? Why had he pulled her on that stage, and why was he being so kind and considerate to her son?

Honestly, she'd figured he'd wave to the crowd and they'd call that a meet and greet. But this...she never would have dreamed.

Melissa found herself a place against the wall and leaned up against it. The room was filled with young girls screaming and chattering. Jesse took pictures with each of his adoring fans and gave them each a moment of his time. Certainly he wasn't stereo-typical to what she'd expected.

"He hates this part."

Melissa looked to find Bryce leaning up against the wall next to her.

"He doesn't look like he hates it too bad."

"It's part of the job. He likes to perform, but all the hype…it's not for him."

Melissa couldn't imagine. Why would someone want to be as famous as Jesse Charles and not like it?

"It's very nice of him to pay attention to Jonah. He really doesn't have to do that."

"I think they have a connection. Jesse's dad died when he was ten. Right about the time he began to perform."

Melissa laid her hand on her chest. Her heart ached every time she heard such a thing. She knew what Jonah was going through. It was bad enough that so many people grew up that way.

"I just hope he's not let down tomorrow. I don't know how to explain to him that people like Jesse don't stick around to be your friend. They pull people on stage and make them feel good for that moment. I understand it, but I don't know how to make him understand it."

"Between you and me, he's never pulled anyone on stage before."

An uneasy feeling had her stomach tightening. "He said that, but I didn't think he meant it."

"He thinks it's tacky."

That still didn't change the fact that tomorrow Jonah would already be missing that moment that Jesse had created for him, and she'd be the one that would have to compensate for another loss in his life.

Melissa would have liked to have left the arena and headed home, but the meet and greet lasted an hour. Jesse had kept Jonah next to him the entire time. Between each overly excited, screaming girl, Jesse would take a moment to talk to Jonah. Melissa laughed aloud when one of the girls even kissed Jonah because he was cute.

When the last of the fans were escorted out of the room Jesse walked back toward her, his arm around Jonah's shoulders.

Jonah's arms were loaded down with posters and T-shirts. And he even wore a new Jesse Charles hat which had been signed.

"Mom, look at all this neat stuff he gave me."

She shook her head. "You really didn't have to do that."

"My pleasure. You have a great kid."

There went her heartbeat, racing at an abnormal pace. "I do have a great kid."

"Mom, can we take a picture on your phone?"

She pulled the smartphone from her pocket and carefully pulled up the camera. The darn thing still made her nervous. It had cost her nearly an entire car payment, but she'd needed it.

She lifted it to take the picture when Bryce rested his hand on her shoulder.

"You go get in there too," he said as he took the phone from her.

She wasn't one to jump into pictures, though she'd always wished she had been. She simply was too critical of herself. Her hair was always a mess, her smile a bit crooked, or God forbid, her hips ended up in the picture. Even at the thought she was thinking she'd start a diet in the morning.

Bryce was still standing there with his hand held open, reaching for the phone.

Melissa handed him the phone and walked toward Jonah and Jesse.

She stood to the side of them, but Jesse slid his arm around her waist and pulled her in closer until they were all three in a tight huddle. There was, however, no way to deny the physical excitement that was pumping through her veins having Jesse Charles pressed close to her; his hand holding firm to her hip and his head pressed against hers.

Bryce looked at the screen on the phone. "That's one cute family pic right there."

That was when all of the excitement and nerves reached her throat and threatened to choke her with tears. Melissa fought them back as she slipped on her coat and handed Jonah his.

Jesse had taken her phone and was looking at the picture. "Do you mind if I send this to myself?"

Melissa had to process the man's words. How could he have gotten her so worked up? She had been worried about Jonah's let down tomorrow when Jesse Charles was just again some news headliner and not someone special—now she wondered how she was going to handle it.

She forced a smile to her face. "Sure."

Jesse hit a few buttons on the phone and then handed it back to her. His own phone buzzed in Bryce's pocket, and he handed it to Jesse.

Jesse pulled up the text on his phone and then showed Jonah the picture. "There. Now I'll never forget tonight."

That had nearly forced the tears to the surface when Melissa saw Jonah's smile. This man was playing with her son's emotions—and hers. She didn't know if she should slap him or kiss him again.

There wasn't much time to process that before Jesse was standing right in front of her, gazing at her with his hypnotic grey eyes.

"Thank you for coming and letting me pull you up on stage."

Her throat had gone dry. "Sure."

He leaned in closer to her. "Thank you for the kiss."

Melissa felt his breath on her cheek and his hand took hold of hers, and he gave it a squeeze before he took a step back and looked down at Jonah.

"See you around, kid. Be good."

"Okay."

Jesse looked back up at Melissa. "Ed is going to walk you out to your car. I don't want anything to happen to you two." He waved, and then he and Bryce slipped into another room as an enormous, burly security guard approached them and walked them out to the parking lot.

Jesse could feel the smile on his face. His cheeks had begun to hurt, and it felt nice to be happy.

Bryce shut the door to the dressing room after having kicked everyone else out of the room.

"What was all of that? You're going to break that little kid's heart."

Jesse dropped down onto the couch in the room and pulled out his phone. "He's fine."

"Why? Because you met him and gave him a few things? Damn, man, you kissed his mother!"

Jesse felt his smile widen. "Yes I did." And it had been a kiss of a lifetime.

"You've been that kid. C'mon, his dad died. Mom obviously works hard to support them and now some spoiled rock star has messed with their heads."

The smile was gone, and Jesse pursed his lips. "That's not my plan."

"You have a plan?"

Jesse pulled up the phone number he'd sent the text to himself from and sent it on in another text and then made a phone call.

"Hey, I need a favor. I know it's the middle of the night. I just texted you a phone number. I need an address by noon."

Jesse turned off his phone and rested his head against the back of the couch.

He had no intentions of letting Jonah down. And whatever it was that turned him inside out when he saw Melissa—he wanted to explore that a little more.

The world was going to think he was crazy. He was twenty-five and tired of being a pop star. There had to be something in his life that meant more.

He thought about the kiss he'd planted on Melissa. He hadn't meant to, but the need to had just taken over. What would it be like to leave it all behind and live a life with her and her son? It was undeniable. There was a spark between them, and just thinking about her made his head spin.

She wasn't a supermodel. Hell, she hardly made it past five foot three, he presumed. She was curvy. Her hair was a mass of uncontrolled curls, and he'd noticed her boots. That part bothered him. Not that he noticed they were old cowboy boots which had seen better days—but that he'd noticed shoes at all. Obviously, he spent way too much time with Bryce.

There had never been a hitch in his heart for a woman as there was with this one.

He'd spent most of his life being admired by people. Certainly he'd be the unexpected admirer when it came to Melissa. But he wasn't going to let it go.

Only a few minutes later, his phone buzzed in his hand. He looked down to see the text message. His connection was fast. There on the screen was Melissa's address.

Jesse took a deep breath and closed his eyes. He had two more shows over the weekend, but maybe Monday he'd take his day off and make a trip back to the beautiful mountains of Colorado.

Chapter Three

It was nearly two o'clock before Melissa's head touched her pillow. All she could hope was that Jonah had quickly fallen asleep when he went to bed. The boy jabbered the entire way home.

It hadn't helped that her mother was up and sitting at the kitchen table when they walked through the door.

"Grandma!" Jonah had yelled. "Jesse Charles kissed mom!"

Her mother's face was priceless, but she didn't say much more. Jonah hadn't given her a chance. He'd told her every detail of the entire night and showed off his *swag*.

He was happy, and that was all that mattered to Melissa.

And now, as she thought of the less than four hours of sleep she desperately needed, that stupid song—which she truly didn't like—played over and over in her head. The melody was only made worse by the memory of Jesse gazing at her when he sang it to her.

She rolled onto her side and pounded at her pillow.

Why had he done that? And why did she care?

She cared because it had been a very long time since a man touched her hand the way he had or had gazed at her to where she'd forgotten where she was.

It was all part of his charm, and she knew that. She'd be a fool to think there had been more, but she couldn't help it.

Finally, she smiled in the dark to herself. It was nice to have a young and attractive man give her some attention. That's all it was, and it was a brief moment in her life. Tomorrow, or later that day, she'd just be Mrs. Mathews again. and that was what she enjoyed most.

She closed her eyes.

But for a moment she was Jesse Charles's girl.

Melissa parked in the parking lot of the school, reached into the car for her bag, her purse, and her lunch box. Then she tried to keep a steady hand on her coffee as she bumped the car door closed with her hip.

She had on her glasses, her eyes much too tired to put in her contacts. The hair dryer had only managed to frizz her hair, and she'd forgotten to write up the test for the end of the unit they would finish in class. The students would be happy about that part.

As she made it to the office, she again readjusted the bags hanging on her arm. There was an angel somewhere as she had yet to spill coffee down the front of her.

She looked at the clock. It was only seven-thirty. Four o'clock was a long ways away.

"You look horrible."

Melissa looked toward William Scott, who stood in the doorway to his office.

"I'm not sure you've ever been that blunt."

"Sorry. Can you come in here?"

Could her morning drag on any more?

Melissa shuffled her way into his office and set her bags in the chair in front of his desk.

William Scott wasn't a threat. He was a dear friend. And as she finally took a sip from her coffee, she reminded herself that she was tired. His snippy comment didn't need to set her mood for the day. Many people did a full day's work on two hours of sleep. She could too.

"How was the concert?"

Melissa let out a long breath. "Loud. Crowded. And, Will, you should have seen Jonah's face." She felt her own cheeks tighten as she smiled.

"He was pretty excited."

"I don't know how he's going to make it through today, but I tell you what...that kid is pumped up."

William nodded his head and sat down in the chair behind his desk. "He deserved a nice night."

"Yes, he did."

"And he met Jesse Charles?"

"Yes. Mr. Charles took very good care of him. He loaded him down with posters, shirts, and a hat." She sipped absent-mindedly at her coffee again and swallowed hard at the bitter taste. "I didn't want to go, but it was an amazing night."

"I'll bet." His words were short, and his gaze narrowed.

"Is something wrong?"

William opened his top desk drawer and pulled out a newspaper. He threw it on the desk for her to see.

Right there, big as life, was a picture of her and Jesse Charles lip locked on stage.

"Oh, my!" The words caught in her throat with a laugh.

William stood and rested his hands on the top of his desk. "This is funny?"

"It's hysterical."

"Are you kidding me?" He stood straight and walked around the desk. "I thought you were going to that concert for Jonah. I thought you won the tickets."

"I did."

"Then how does my best teacher end up in the newspaper kissing some kid?"

She didn't like how that sounded at all. Melissa tossed the paper back on the desk and turned toward William.

"Listen, I didn't want to go. I went for Jonah, and you know it. The man sent for me so he could sing to me. He saw me in the crowd."

"You?"

"Well, don't act so surprised. Martin thought I was good enough."

William ran his hand over his hair. "I didn't mean it that way."

She knew that, but it didn't make it any easier to deal with. "I went on stage. He sang to me and then he kissed me. End of story. Backstage he showed Jonah around and kept him by his side. It was just what Jonah needed."

William reached for her arm and lingered his hand there. "I'm sorry. You're right. Jonah deserved such a great night. I'm out of line."

"You're looking out for us. You always have."

"I promised Martin I would."

Melissa nodded reached down to pick up her bags. William moved in quicker. "I'll get these."

"Thank you."

He picked up the bags, and together they headed toward the science lab.

Melissa unlocked the door and stepped inside the room. William followed her as she turned on the light.

"How are we going to deal with this?" he asked as he set her bags on her desk.

"Deal with what?"

"The kiss? The paper?"

Melissa laughed. "Nothing is going to come of it. And if it does, it'll be over by the end of the day and old news by Monday. Let it go."

"Dinner Sunday?"

The man was all over the place today.

"Why don't you come by. Mom is making spaghetti."

His cheeks rose when she mentioned it. "I'll be there. I haven't had Patty's sauce in a long time."

"Not since last month."

He chuckled and started for the door when the first student nearly pushed him over as she ran into the classroom.

"Mrs. Mathews, O-M-G you kissed Jesse Charles!"

Melissa sucked in air, but it stuck in her lungs as she saw William's eyes narrow as he walked out of the room.

She let the breath out slowly. It was going to be a very long day.

When the last student walked out of Melissa's room for the day, she dropped her head on the desk. If she could just make it to her car without one more person mentioning the fact that they had either seen her pulled on stage and kissed, or read it in the paper—or worse, heard about it on the news—then life might feel normal. She was exhausted, and the day had certainly not held any educational merit.

Melissa lifted her head, ready to leave and go home, only to find the art teacher standing in her door, grinning widely.

"I thought maybe you'd fallen asleep."

Melissa forced a grin, but looking at the petite and very young teacher who stood in front of her, she'd rather just growl.

Emmy Lou Grant was a free spirit with a flowing skirt and arms full of D.Y.I. bracelets. Every ounce of her screamed *beautiful on the inside and out*, and at that moment, Melissa hated that very charming trait.

Melissa stood from her chair and blew a wayward curl from her eyes. "I think I'm going to head home and curl into a ball under a blanket until Sunday."

Emmy Lou nodded, but the grin on her face said she had more to discuss.

"I saw you at the concert last night," she whispered as if she didn't know the entire world knew about her flash stardom.

Melissa took another look at her, and envy sliced through her. How was it they were at the same concert, taught the same kids, and yet Melissa was sure she looked as disheveled as she felt and Emmy Lou Grant still had a fairy's glow to her?

"You were there, huh?" She began to pick up the papers on her desk and stuff them into her bag.

"Oh, I don't miss a Jesse Charles concert if it's within two-hundred miles."

Now the thought of age crept into Melissa's head. How young was this spirited woman before her?

Emmy Lou walked fully into the room and right up to her desk. "I've never seen him do that before."

"Do what?"

"Pull someone up on stage."

"And you've seen him a lot?"

Emmy Lou tapped her fingers together in a self-applause. The bangles on her arms clamored together. "I've seen him twenty-seven times."

Melissa couldn't help it. She choked out a laugh. "You're a big fan, huh?"

"Card carrying." Emmy Lou picked up a bobble head frog from the edge of Melissa's desk and bopped the head. She grinned as it danced in her hands. "Anyway, what made him do that?"

Melissa shoved another stack of papers into the bag. "I don't know. Maybe he was high."

Emmy Lou's expression changed immediately. Her eyes widened and finally Melissa saw a line form between her brows as Emmy Lou quickly set the frog back on the desk.

"He doesn't do drugs."

"Oh." How was she supposed to respond to that? This girl was as crazy as the kids when it came to this man.

"He's very anti-drugs, and that is why he's sort of a joke to other artists."

Melissa wanted to laugh at how serious this conversation had turned. The point was, she didn't care. All she wanted was Monday to roll around so she could just be the mean science teacher with a test and not the girl Jesse Charles kissed.

"I'm sure he's a great guy. I don't know what motivated him to pull me on stage. A joke, I assume. But, it's over now and I can get back to my life." She hoisted the bag over her shoulder.

"All I wanted to say was you're a very lucky girl. From where I was perched, he looked really into you."

Really into her? Maybe Emmy Lou was high. The thought made her chuckle.

"Maybe he changed how he does things."

Emmy Lou shrugged her shoulders and walked back across the room toward the door. "Well, I just wanted to tell you that you looked beautiful last night, and he must have noticed. It must feel nice to have the attention of two very nice looking men."

"Two?"

"Jesse Charles, of course." Emmy Lou looked down the hall as if to make sure it were clear and then she turned back to Melissa. "And William Scott."

She could feel her face drain of color as Emmy Lou waved and walked away.

What was that to have meant? Of course, she had William's attention. He was Martin's best friend. He'd taken on a father role to Jonah and—oh!—and a very supportive husband-like role to her.

Dear Lord, did the entire school assume they were involved?

The day escalated from horrible to catastrophic.

Melissa hurried to shut her door and lock it. Just as she turned around William turned the corner, and she ran right into his chest with her face.

She dropped the bag of papers, and they scattered all over the floor.

She couldn't help but stomp her feet like a child before she knelt down to gather them back into the bag.

William dropped to his knees and began to help. "Is everything okay?"

"Lousy day."

"Tell me about it." He reached for a paper at the same time she did.

Their hands touched, and she flinched. She dropped the paper and went to another, but she caught the edge and reared back. "Ouch!"

"Paper cut?"

She nodded as a small dot of blood surfaced on her finger. She wiped it clean and gave it a shake.

"Let me see." He took her hand, in the same manner he would have yesterday or the day before. He looked it over and then placed a kiss on the cut.

Melissa sat back on her heels and stared at him. She'd never seen it. She'd been an idiot, and now she knew that there was some underground rumor mill brewing.

William stuffed the last of the papers into the bag and looked at her. "Are you feeling okay?"

"Fine." She jumped to her feet and grabbed the bag from his hand. "I have to go."

She tried to dart around him, but he caught her arm. "Are you up for dancing tomorrow? We haven't done that in a long time, and there's a great band playing in Aspen Hills tomorrow."

Her heartbeat kicked up, and she could feel the sweat on her brow. This wasn't what she wanted. William was a friend. Why had she never seen this?

"No. I have a lot of work. In fact, I think I'm going to be very busy all weekend. So maybe we can reschedule dinner on

Sunday for some other time, too. I have a test to write and…"

She was trying to walk away, but he was following her.

"I could help you grade."

"Nope. I'm fine. I have to go."

She all but sprinted out of the school, leaving behind the man who had never been anything but nice to her and had taken care of her.

Melissa hurried to the car and threw her bag in the passenger seat. She slid in behind the wheel and started the engine. When she looked up, William was still at the door to the school. He gave a wave, and she sped out of the parking lot.

She was tired. That was all it was. She needed a full night's sleep and then maybe things would make more sense because, as it was, she wasn't sure, but she might have dropped into some parallel universe. Nothing made sense anymore after that kiss from Jesse Charles.

Chapter Four

As Melissa had expected, things had eased up over the weekend.

She'd graded papers on Saturday and helped her mother with the sauce she was going to can. They'd taken a trip to the nursing home to visit her grandfather, and after church on Sunday, she and Jonah sat down to watch the Bronco game.

She didn't much like football, but Martin had. It had been one of those father and son bonding things that she'd taken over when Martin died.

Jonah enjoyed trying to explain the game to her. She had to admit she was getting it, slowly. But it was more important that they were making their own memories and carrying on in Martin's memory.

Monday morning Melissa had convinced Jonah that if he hurried out of the house a few minutes early, she'd take him by Molly's coffee shop for a muffin. She knew it was a sure fire way to get him moving, and it had worked. In reality, she wanted to get situated in her room and have a few minutes to prepare before her students filed in.

Molly's was already bustling, just as it did every morning. The residents of Aspen Creek appreciated the quaint gathering place as well as the fantastic coffees and baked goods.

Melissa placed her order and stood to the side of the counter to wait for it to be served up. When the door to the shop opened again, the man who walked through gave her a gracious nod.

She returned the gesture. "Hey, Cade. Heading in early too?"

"Yup. Big game coming up on Saturday. I have a week to pull together some good plays."

She watched him as he ordered his coffee and another, decaf coffee to go. No doubt for his wife.

Melissa had grown up down the street from Cade Carter and his wife, Olivia Baker. They never ran in the same crowds, but her memories of growing up in the small town certainly included them. Wouldn't Martin be surprised to find that Cade and Olivia had actually married. Even more surprising would be the fact that Cade had come back to the small town he'd abandoned when he became a professional football player.

"How is Olivia feeling?" Melissa asked as she picked up the bag with Jonah's muffin and handed it to him.

"She's feeling very done with being pregnant," he laughed. "Otherwise, she's feeling great and Gage is ready to meet his brother."

"I heard you're going to name him after your father?"

Cade nodded. "Yep. He really raised us both and made sure we found each other. It only seems right."

"It sure does." Molly handed her the coffee she had ordered. Melissa lifted it to her nose and took a sniff. It was just what she needed. "Give Olivia my best."

Cade walked off and Melissa looked around the enormous parking lot. All three schools sat in the same corner of Aspen Creek. The elementary teachers had parked and the kids were beginning to arrive. The middle school lot was filling up and soon the high schoolers would begin arriving in their own cars.

There was a time when martin would sit out front of the school in his patrol car just to keep absent minded teenagers in check.

The memory stung and Melissa's heart ached. She missed him.

Three years hadn't eased the pain of him being gone. She twisted the band of gold which still adorned her finger. He was too young, she was too young—Jonah was too young to be without him.

"Mom, Todd is already at school. Can I run over there?" Jonah pleaded.

Melissa looked across the parking lot and Sandy Sharp, the town's most loved kindergarten teacher, waved back. She signaled to them to send Jonah over.

"Go, but you stay out of Mrs. Sharp's way. And get to your own class on time."

"Got it." He turned to run off.

"Oh, no you don't. Give me a kiss."

Jonah turned back to her and narrowed his eyes. "I'll see you in like six hours."

"Yep, and this will get me through my day."

Reluctantly he kissed her on the cheek and then took off in a flash to be with his friend. She gave Sandy a grateful wave and headed into the school.

The office was quiet, and William's door was closed.

Melissa hurried to fetch her papers and get to her classroom. There were going to be eighty students who would be facing a test today, and she knew she'd be on the least popular list. This was a place she was more comfortable. All the silliness and wasted time of Friday was over. It was time to move on—back to normality.

The last bell of the day rang, and as the students hurried out of her room, Melissa laid her head on the desk.

"That test must have been as bad as I heard," William's voice rang through the room.

Melissa lifted her head to see him leaned up against the door jamb.

She'd avoided him for an entire weekend and the whole school day. It had been stupid to think that he'd never try to talk to her again just because she gave him the cold shoulder. William Scott was her friend. Perhaps it only made sense that maybe he had feelings for her.

"Not only did I give them all a test and they grumbled about it, but now I have to grade them." She ran her hands through her matted curls.

William walked into the room and right toward her desk where he sat down on the corner of it. "I'd love to help you with that."

Before Emmy Lou had walked in last week with her accusations, this would have been normal. She would have accepted his generosity and never have noticed the gaze he gave her.

Melissa shuffled the papers together and stacked them. "I think I'll be fine."

William stood, but he was still much too close to her. He touched her arm. "Is everything okay? I feel as though I'm being brushed off. I'm not sure what I did."

Melissa let out a sigh. "I'm sorry. I'm just a bit out of sorts this week."

He reached up to her hair and ran his hand over it. "You're still tired from your concert night."

She reached for his hand. Again, it shouldn't have been awkward. This man had been by her side for three years and a dear friend long before Martin had died. Why only now did she notice how he looked at her? Had there never been any personal boundaries? Did he always touch her like that? It was no wonder people talked.

"I think you're right. I'm just tired." She shoved the stack of papers into her bag. "I'd better get home."

"My offer still stands. I don't mind grading biology papers."

"I'll call you if I get in a bind."

As she pulled away from the school she could see the high school football team up on the field. She smiled when she saw Cade on the sidelines, his son Gage on his hip.

Sadness enveloped her again. Jonah would miss all of that. William had stepped in and done everything he could for Jonah. He'd taken him to Cub Scouts and to the auxiliary's father/son spaghetti dinners. But it wasn't the same. Jonah had a father and in one moment that was taken away.

The ache in her chest deepened.

She too missed having someone hold her at night, make plans with, and just happily exist side by side. She and Martin had had plans. They'd wanted a house full of children. There had been trips to take and parties to throw. How had it been taken from her so quickly?

Melissa drove through town and over the Rose Bridge heading home to her son and mother. That was the normal now, and she would continue to make the very best of it.

As she turned down the street, her house came into view, but something was not right. There was a black pickup truck parked across the street. She'd never seen the truck before, and in a small town, little things like trucks parked on streets stood out. As she pulled into the driveway, she noticed a man was sitting in the truck, and he was looking her way. He rolled down the window as she climbed out of the car.

The ache in her chest became a flurry of panic. Her mother and son—what if something happened to them? Why was this man parked outside her house?

She knew it wasn't the best idea to even leave the security of her car, but motherly instincts took over.

Melissa hurried from the car and straight through the front door of the house. As she stepped over the threshold, her grip on the door handle slipped. The door slammed into the wall, and she fell to her knees.

"Melissa!" she heard her mother's voice ring through the house.

When she looked up she saw her mother and Jonah standing above her. They were fine.

But there was someone else standing above her looking down at her on her knees, which now ached against the tile floor.

Jesse Charles?

Jesse reached a hand toward her to help her up. She took his hand and stood.

"Are you okay?" His voice was soft.

"Yeah."

Melissa gave a glance to her mother and son, who stood there smiling.

Her mother moved closer to her. "Why were you busting through the door? My goodness, girl, what were you thinking?"

"There's a truck…outside." She caught her breath and turned back to Jesse. "Why are you here?"

"Melissa!" her mother scolded. "Is this how you greet your guest?"

"Guest?"

He was flashing that brilliant smile again. "I had a few days off from my tour, and I thought I'd drop by for a visit."

"How did you find me?"

"I texted myself the picture the other night so I had your phone number." He looked at her son and then back to her. "I'm sorry to have just dropped by." His smile had gone. "I should have called."

Jonah moved in between them. "Mom, he came to take you to dinner."

"Dinner? I can't go to dinner. I have tests to grade."

"Oh." Jesse tucked his thumbs into the front pockets of his jeans. "I really should have called."

"Nonsense," her mother injected. "Melissa, a nice man stopped by to take you to dinner. You go. Those tests will wait."

She was very sure she had crossed over into some parallel universe. What was Jesse Charles doing in her house?

"The man...outside."

"Bodyguard." He grinned, but there was a flush to his cheeks. Did that embarrass him?

"You brought your bodyguard with you?"

"What if you *really* didn't want to see me and met me at the door with a shotgun?"

"Maybe you'd deserve it."

"Melissa!" Her mother's voice again rose in pitch and volume.

She felt the heat creep into her cheeks now. Here she was, thirty-five years old, and her mother was scolding her.

"I'm sorry. This is just about the oddest thing that has ever happened to me." She took a deep breath. "You came to take us to dinner?"

Jonah reached for her hand. "Mom, he came to take *you* to dinner."

She looked down at him, and he was smiling again. What was it about this man that could make her son smile so much?

"Grandma and I will be fine," he assured her. "We have lots to eat. You go with Jesse."

Jesse stepped in closer to her. "I won't keep you long, I promise. I know you have a lot of work to do."

Melissa's emotions were conflicted. She had a duty as a teacher to finish those tests and to get to bed on time. She had obligations as a mother to keep silly delusions out of her son's head—such as his mother going on a date with some younger man, who just happened to be one of the most famous men in America. But on the other hand, here was a man, standing in her living room, gazing at her with the most hypnotic grey eyes. She wanted to spend some time with him. After all, she already knew how he kissed.

She took a deep breath and placed her hands on her jumpy stomach. She looked down at her outfit. How was it that Jesse Charles stood there looking at her with dreamy eyes as though he hadn't even noticed the vest she wore had adorned frogs?

"Let me get changed."

Melissa quickly changed into a nice pair of jeans and a pair of shoes she wouldn't normally wear in November, but this certainly wasn't her normal weeknight. She fussed with her hair for only a moment—there just wasn't much more she could do with it. She added some lipstick and decided that if he'd seen her fresh off work, falling through the front door, and he'd still smiled as though he wanted to continue an evening with her, then it was good enough.

Jesse was on the couch helping Jonah with his math homework when she walked out of her room. The moment he saw her he stood. Somewhere the young man had been taught manners. That was a plus.

He walked toward her. "You look wonderful."

She wasn't sure how he'd noticed. He'd never looked at her body, only her eyes.

"Thank you." Her voice waivered. That wasn't a good sign.

Her mother opened the front door. "I called Mama's and talked to Ramone. He has a table for you already."

One thing about Patsy Bartlett, she was always thinking one step ahead.

Though the residents of Aspen Creek were used to the occasional "famous person" coming over from Aspen Hills for the quiet serenity of their small town, someone as popular as Jesse Charles, was going to cause a stir.

"Thank you."

She pulled her jacket off of the rack by the door, and Jesse moved in to help her. "I hope you don't mind, but would you drive? If we take my truck, he'll have to go with us." He nodded toward the man sitting in the truck out front of the house.

"Sure." Again her voice rattled in her throat.

She'd never minded her small car until that very moment. The once very pretty, black Toyota Camry looked dull and old. She'd never needed anything more, even if the winters were tough. But it was paid for.

Jesse opened her door and waited for her to slip in behind the wheel before he shut it and walked around to the other side to get in.

"So Mama's? Is that Italian?"

She chuckled. "If you could call it that. Premade noodles and sauce, but Mama Lombardi says it's homemade."

"I see." He buckled his seat belt. "But your mom must like it?"

"They have a good pizza." She turned the key to start the engine. and it hiccupped. She tried again, and this time it started.

Melissa backed out of the driveway and headed down the street toward the bridge. She noticed in the mirror that the truck, which had been parked out front of her house, was following them.

"Is he going to follow us to the restaurant?"

Jesse turned back and looked. "Yep. That's how it works."

"So you're never alone?"

The corners of his mouth turned down. "No."

That was as pathetic as it came in her book. Sure, she always had Jonah and her mother nearby, but on Sunday morning even she'd head down to Molly's for a cup of coffee after church for a moment to herself. What would it be like if someone had to follow your every move?

Jesse pulled a CD from the holder attached to her visor. "Tim McGraw?"

"What?" She glanced toward him and then back to the road. "Oh, yeah."

"Country girl?"

"That's my preference." An uncomfortable tightness grew in her chest.

"I saw them in Vegas, he and his wife. Nice people."

The thought caught her as funny. "I'll bet you've met a lot of people."

"Sure. Most of them are shallow and all about themselves. I like things more laid back."

"Well, you're in the right place for that. Aspen Creek is almost too laid back."

"Do you really think so?" He adjusted in his seat. "On my way into town, I saw a tanning salon, an ice rink boasting of hockey tryouts on a sign, a yoga studio, and a gourmet coffee place. This isn't what I'd have in mind for small town. Oh, and that sign as you drive in," he paused and looked at her for acknowledgement, and she nodded. "Cade Carter is from here?"

"He coaches the football team."

"Isn't that something? I remember that game when he got hit. Ended his career."

She turned down Main Street. "I suppose that depends on how you look at it. Without that injury, he wouldn't have come home to fall in love with the girl he grew up next door to, and they have a beautiful son and one on the way."

"Hmmm." Jesse looked out the window and then back at her. "And Lillian Rose? She's an actress from early Hollywood, right?"

Melissa couldn't help but smile. "Yes. The bridge we crossed to come into town is named after her family." She stopped at the stop sign and pointed out the window. "And, do you see that house up on the mountain?"

"Yeah, I see it."

"That's where she was born in a blizzard. Her father died in the blizzard, and her mother eventually married her uncle. Huge love story there. But right below it, oh midway down the mountain, do you see that big, red barn?"

Jesse moved his head around to get the best view. "Okay, I see it."

"That's my grandfather's land. My mother grew up there, and I lived there for years myself."

"That's cool."

Melissa pulled into the parking lot of the Italian restaurant, and the black truck pulled in right beside her.

Jesse took a deep breath and let his shoulders drop. "I like it here. L.A. is just fully of people trying to impress other people."

"I think you'll find that wherever you go."

"So far, this is more my pace." He smiled and climbed out of the car.

Before she could unbuckle her seat belt, he was at her door opening it for her.

"Thank you."

"My pleasure."

Ramone Lombardi walked out of the door on the side of the restaurant and waved. "Ah, your mother said you'd be coming, and you had a very special guest."

"Ramone, this is Jesse."

Jesse held his hand out to shake Ramone's hand. "It's nice to meet you, sir."

"Oh, what a gentleman. Come, I have a table set up for you."

He led them through the side door and through the kitchen. Ramone hadn't said anything to Jesse about knowing who he was, but he had kept his composure and guided them to a table just off the kitchen where they wouldn't be bothered by the other diners.

The booths had high backs, and unless someone came right to the table, no one would even know they were there. She owed her mother for that. Melissa knew what the scene would be otherwise. There would be mass hysteria in the small town. In fact, as soon as the word got out that he was in their small town, she assumed there would still be some pandemonium.

As she sat down in the booth, she looked at the man next to her. There still was no reasoning behind why she was sitting in a restaurant with him. The flash of a smile which had crossed her son's face was the only reason she was out with the stranger who had stalked her from a text message.

The thought was funny to her, and Jesse must have noticed.

"What's so funny?"

"Did I laugh out loud?"

"With your eyes," he said as he settled into the booth.

She sighed and settled into the booth, pulling her jacket from her arms and wiggling out of it. "Sorry. I'm still not sure why you're here, and why I'm sitting in some booth with you. Do you take out all the women you sing to?"

His lips pursed as he pulled his jacket off. "I've never pulled anyone up on stage before."

"I find that hard to believe," she said defensively, though she didn't mean to be so snide.

Jesse folded his jacket and set it on the seat next to him. He then rested his arms on the table and leaned in. "Why is it so hard to accept that a man wanted to have dinner with you?"

"Because the man is you, and the woman is me."

"So."

"So?" She looked around and noticed that a few of the wait staff had noticed who she was with, and Ramone shooed them away. "So, I'm probably fifteen years older than you, for one."

"I'm twenty-six."

She did the math. "Okay, seven, but…"

"But what? I think you're wonderful."

"You just met me."

"And at one time in your life hadn't you just met your husband?"

The wind was taken out of her sails with that. "Yes."

"A stranger is just a friend you haven't met yet."

Suddenly she felt as though her teacher credentials meant nothing, and this "kid" knew more than she did. "Why me?"

Jesse sat back against the booth. "Why did I pull you on stage?"

"Yes."

"Because you didn't fit in the audience."

Melissa pushed her shoulders back. "What does that mean?"

Jesse smiled and crossed his arms over his chest. "I mean, you're not a fan of my music."

"And you're here to try and make me a fan?"

He leaned in again. "Not of my music."

Ramone approached the table. "How about a beer?"

Jesse looked at her for her decision, and she felt panic rise in her chest. "How about a Coke."

"I'll have the same," Jesse said.

Ramone gave a nod and walked away.

Jesse eased back against the back of the booth. "You don't drink?"

"Not with men I don't know."

Jesse gave a slow nod. "Are you going to give this a chance?"

"Dinner?"

"Any of it." Jesse reached across the table and took hold of her hands. "Listen, I don't want you to think any more about this than us getting to know each other. I saw you. I like you. I want to get to know you."

"Jesse, I haven't dated anyone since my husband died."

He sat back again. "Maybe would could be friends."

She was being foolish. Perhaps she did deserve to be scolded by her mother.

Ramone returned with their drinks, and they agreed on a pizza for dinner.

"So," Jesse began and then took a sip of his Coke. "You're a country fan?"

She smiled. "My father and my husband were big Johnny Cash fans."

"*Man in Black*. You can't go wrong with Cash."

Melissa considered him for a moment. "You like Johnny Cash?"

"He's classic. He's one of the foundations of modern music." He leaned on the table again. "Imagine if the world hadn't had Johnny Cash, or Elvis Presley, or even Glenn Miller. If the classic tones of Beethoven and Mozart hadn't led to something new…" He sat back in his seat and let out a breath. "It's all combined. Without one, you don't have the other. To not appreciate one…well, that's just sad."

She hadn't expected such passion from him. "And Justin Beiber?"

"That is one talented S.O.B."

She laughed at that. Talk about a controversy when you got two thirteen year olds going at it in the hall.

"What made you want to sing?"

He sipped his Coke, and his lips pursed. "My mother. She married a musician, and then had a kid with a musician. She saw easy street if she made her kid one, too."

"You didn't choose this?"

He shrugged his shoulders. "It's all I've ever known. I was auditioning for things by the time I was eight. I auditioned for *The Guys* when I was ten. They hired me when I was twelve. I sang with them until I was eighteen, and then I went solo. The rest is history."

"I forgot you sang in a boy band."

He winced as if the title hurt. "Yep. Seems like a long time ago."

"What would you rather have done?"

This time he smiled, and she knew that was half his charm. She was fairly sure he knew it too. "I would have like to have played baseball."

"Professionally?"

The smile began to diminish. "No. Just little league. You know, with kids from school. Dirt lots, faded baseball caps, ratty glove." His eyes glazed over when he spoke of it.

"You never got to do that?"

He picked up his drink again. "No. Mom was looking for a record contract and where she went, I went."

Melissa's heart ached for him. Sure, Martin wasn't around to do those things with Jonah, but he played basketball. One spring he'd played T-ball, and he'd already asked if he could try hockey when the season started the following year.

"Are you happy?"

"Sure." He said the words, but Melissa didn't buy it.

Ramone set their pizza down on the table and hurried away, again shooing his young wait staff.

Jesse served her a piece and then himself. "This looks great."

"Best in the county."

He took his first bite. "Yep, that's good."

"So how did you know I wasn't at the concert to listen to you?"

"Because your eyes were on the crowd. You didn't always sing along, but you smiled. So it wasn't as if you'd been completely forced there."

"You can really see people like that?"

He swallowed his bite and wiped the cheese from his chin. "There are the hard core fans, the ones who feel as though they personally know you. There are the ones who come scantily dressed, hoping you'll take them backstage, and then usually get drunk and go home with someone they don't know. There are the kids, like Jonah, who just enjoy the music. I like them the best." He smiled. "But then there are those who are there only because someone dragged them along. They are miserable, and they do make eye contact with you. Only it's a demented look as though you've wrecked their life."

She chuckled as she bit into her pizza. "And me?"

"You were defiantly there because you came with someone you cared about. You were having a good time, but you wouldn't have been there if someone hadn't needed a ride."

She wiped her mouth and tried to hide the knowing grin she knew had surfaced.

Jesse reached across the table and touched her arm. "You finally looked up at the stage and caught my eye. We connected, did you feel it?"

She felt the blood drain from her head. "I thought I was crazy."

He shook his head. "I've never had that happen before. That's why I made them bring you on stage. I wanted to see you up close."

"I thought it was all part of the show."

"I've never done that before."

Bryce had told her that, but she hadn't really believed it. "I don't understand. I'm older than you. I'm widowed. I have a son. I teach middle school biology…"

"You're beautiful. Your eyes show your sensitivity. You're not perfect, and I mean that in the most sincere way. You have to believe me. I live in L.A. I enjoy the freshness of you."

She wasn't sure it was a compliment, but his eyes reached into her soul, and she knew he was speaking from the heart.

"What do you want?" Her voice shook.

"I want to get to know you. Melissa, I know it's crazy and this isn't the circumstances in which you probably thought you'd meet someone, but I really do want to get to know you."

"My son is too impressionable. I don't want him getting a big head that you're here. What happens when you're gone? When I'm just some has-been to you? I'm not the kind to give myself to a man…"

"I'm not asking you to."

"I can't do this to Jonah."

Jesse sat back. "I understand that."

She waited for him to argue with her, but he didn't. "You do?"

"Sure. My mom has been married six times. I met my dad when I was six, and he died when I was ten. I've lived in eight cities and…" He paused and looked up as though he were thinking and then continued, "twenty…no, twenty-one houses. I went to five elementary schools and was tutored through high school. I never went to prom or had a letterman's jacket. Normal is what Jonah needs."

Melissa wasn't sure what she felt now, but there was a great deal of sorrow in her heart for the boyhood that was lost. Maybe Jesse Charles needed some normality, too.

"So where do you go when you leave here?"

He thought for a moment. "Let's see, I just finished in Salt Lake, so I'm in Kansas City tomorrow night, Dallas on Wednesday, and New Orleans on Saturday."

She was exhausted just listening to him. "You travel that much all the time?"

"Part of the job."

"For how much longer?"

"The tour ends the first part of December in L.A.."

There was a pang of regret in her heart. For a moment she'd considered letting him into her life, even if just for a moment of normality in a pizza restaurant in a small town, but his life was too busy to include her and it was certainly too chaotic to make Jonah part of it.

"Maybe when things settle down for you, you could drop back through town. Jonah would really like to see you again."

Again, he reached across the table and this time he took hold of her hands. "I was hoping maybe I could fly back out next Sunday. I bought the truck to have in town and…"

"The black pickup? You bought that to have here?"

"I was hoping to get a lot of use out of it."

Now she didn't know whether to be honored or feel shocked. "So what was your plan?"

His eyes softened, and he ran his thumb over her knuckles. "I was hoping to fly back out here and see you again. Maybe, if you didn't mind, you could cook me dinner. I'm dying for a home-cooked meal. And I'd love to get to spend some time with both you and Jonah."

She swallowed hard. "And my mother. She lives with us."

"Even better."

"I don't think this is a good idea." She didn't know why she felt the need to tell him that, but it was what she felt.

"Will you give me one more day? Melissa, I really want to get to know you."

"Shouldn't you be dating a super model? Or isn't there some diva who needs a good looking man?"

He sat back and laughed. "Well, at least you think I'm good looking."

She sure did, and it seemed to be the driving force in her forgetting her common sense.

Jesse shook Ramone's hand as he let them out the side door. There was a great appreciation for the respect the man had shown them as they dined.

He'd seen the way Ramone had kept the girls in the back away from their table and a few others who had spotted them in the restaurant.

Perhaps it would give him a little more leverage with Melissa. He seemed nearly desperate for her to want to be with him.

He opened the car door for her and waited until she climbed in. Then he skirted to the front of the truck, gave a wave to Paul, the guard in the truck who Ramone had graciously fed as well, and then climbed into her car.

When she started the engine, it growled before it finally gave in.

"Sounds like it doesn't like the cold."

She shook her head. "This is what happens when you pay off a car. Then it wants to quit on you."

"I could look at it for you next weekend."

She chuckled and shifted her eyes toward him in the dark. "You can fix cars?"

Now it was his turn to laugh. "No. I have no idea about cars, but I thought it would give me another reason to come back."

Melissa rested her head against the seat. "You really want to do this? You really want to come back? I'm nothing but a dull, ordinary woman."

"You're exactly the woman I want to be with."

"I'm afraid I'll disappoint you."

He moved in closer to her and cupped her face in his hands. "I can't imagine that you will."

It was time to give her something to remember him by. He caressed her cheek and then moved his fingers into her hair as he pulled her closer. He'd expected her to pull away, but she moved closer to him. Her breath grew heavier and her eyes closed as he pressed his lips to hers.

He'd kissed so many women in his life, and there was nothing compared to the spark he felt when he kissed Melissa.

Her lips had grown softer, and he took the kiss deeper. She accepted, and he let his tongue part her lips.

There was a moan that escaped from one of them, but he wasn't so sure it hadn't come from him.

Melissa's hands moved to his chest. His heartbeat ramped up as the heat from her palms penetrated the cloth of his shirt and warmed his skin.

When she finally broke contact, she didn't move away completely, and they were both breathless.

"That was dangerous," she said as she tried to catch her breath.

"Why?"

"I haven't kissed anyone like that in…"

"I've never kissed anyone like that." He sat back. "It was nice."

She gazed at him for a moment. "Yes. It was."

"You'll let me come back and visit next weekend?"

She thought about it for a moment. "Don't hurt Jonah."

The words pierced his heart, but he understood her concern. "I won't hurt him."

Melissa sighed. "I hope you like spaghetti. It's one of the only things I know how to make and not screw up."

There was no doubt in his mind it was going to be the best meal he'd ever have. Now all he had to do was break the news to his manager that he wouldn't be meeting the *date* he'd set up for him. He didn't want to meet anyone else. He wanted Melissa, the biology teacher from Aspen Creek.

Chapter Five

There was no doubt in Melissa's mind that there was a particularly new spring in her step as she walked into the front office of the school and collected her papers from her box.

"Mornin'," William said from his office.

She smiled and replied, "Mornin'."

There was nothing much she had to say to him so she collected her items and walked out of the office, but as she'd figured would be the case, he was right behind her.

"I came by last night to help you grade those tests."

"I told you I didn't need any help."

She was walking faster down the hall, and he was keeping in step with her. "Your mom said you were on a date."

"She did, huh?" Melissa took the key from her pocket and unlocked her classroom door.

She pushed it open and stepped through, but William didn't just walk in with her. As she turned on the light, he shut the door.

"I heard you were out with that rock star."

"Pop star, big difference you know." The grin on her lips was hurting her cheeks, but she was enjoying the sight of William losing his composure.

"This is ridiculous and has gone on too long."

Melissa set her bags on her desk. "You're ridiculous. Why are you so worked up?"

"Do you think Martin would approve of this?"

Her jaw clenched, and she was very aware that the smile had left her lips. "Martin is dead, and for three years I've played the dutiful wife to his memory. Look," she said as she held her hand up, "I've never taken this ring off since he gave it to me. I didn't go and change my name. I've never dated. A nice young man wants to spend some time with me. I think I'm entitled."

William moved in toward her and rested his hands on her desk. "What about Jonah? This is good for him?"

"He likes Jesse."

"Jesse? You're on a first name basis with him?"

"I kissed him too. Are you going to fire me?" Her voice had risen much higher than she'd hoped it would.

Their argument was interrupted by a knock at the door, and Emmy Lou stepped into the room with an enormous bouquet of roses.

"These came for you. I told them I was going to walk by your room, and I'd bring them. I think there are three dozen roses in here. Morning, Mr. Scott," she said all in one breath.

"Thank you." Melissa walked across the room and took them from her. "Oh, they're beautiful."

Emmy Lou leaned in as Melissa took the vase from her. "Do you think they're from *him?* I heard he was in town and took you to dinner."

Melissa hadn't expected anything less than for it to be common knowledge, but hearing it from someone other than a very worked up William Scott made her stomach drop.

"I assume so. Thank you." She hoped her tone would shoo Emmy Lou away, but she remained.

William stood straight and crossed his arms over his chest. The room grew tense, and Melissa thought if one of them didn't leave soon, she would.

Emmy Lou rose up on her toes and back down as she sucked in some of the stale air that was clogging up the room. "I'd better get back to my classroom. Art club starts tomorrow, and I have to get the projects together. Macramé. An art that's coming back. You know you can pin some great designs on Pinterest." She waved and finally walked out of the room.

William huffed out a breath. "That woman talks way too much."

"She likes you. You should be nice."

"Likes me?"

Melissa's smile had returned. She could feel it down to her toes. "Yes. As in she thinks you're very handsome."

"The women in this town have lost their minds."

The bell rang and Melissa could hear the unmistakable sound of kids filling the halls. She set the flowers behind her desk on the file cabinet as William headed toward the door.

"I still don't like this. I think you're going to cause problems if you see him again."

"Problems for who, William?"

"Yourself and your son. But think of the students, too. You're giving them unrealistic expectations for life. *Pop stars* don't always just show up for you and want to whisk you away. There are consequences for every action, Melissa, and you have a responsibility."

He stormed out of the room, leaving her with a pang of guilt in her chest and the smell of floral beauty reminding her that he was right. Dinner with Jesse would have to be the end of this silly affair.

The door pushed open, and her class began to assemble. But the usual Monday morning banter had already turned into mummers among the girls.

When the final bell rang, Melissa picked up the stack of tests to hand back. One of the girls in the back of the room, who looked as though she were just about to burst, spoke up. "Mrs. Mathews, did you really go on a date with Jesse Charles last night?"

Before she could speak, a boy in the front piped up. "My dad's cousin in Grand Junction sold him a truck so he could keep it in town."

"My sister was working at the restaurant and saw you there with him," another girl said.

"He's a tool," the boy to her left gave as his opinion. "He's got that supermodel girlfriend. What would he want her for?" He motioned to Melissa.

She took a breath to speak, but the class continued on without her.

"He's not dating that model," a girl with a Jesse Charles folder on her desk defended. "That is made up."

"Whatever. He can *have* anyone he wants. Why would he choose Mrs. Mathews?" The boy turned to look at her. "No offense. You're just not his type."

William had been right. She could smell the roses behind her, and her stomach churned at the scent. Supermodels, musicians, and biology teachers from small towns didn't mix well.

When would the life in this parallel universe end?

She turned around and threw the tests in the trash. She heard the gasps from behind her.

"Let's learn some biology. Clean slate. But the next test will be harder."

Now she felt in control again.

Melissa had hurried away from the school as fast as she could when the day was over. The last thing she wanted to hear was another thirteen-year-old asking her if Jesse Charles was a good kisser.

Romances in small towns were hard enough when both people were normal, but when one was famous, it was proving to be nearly impossible.

The rumor mill had started, and her greater concern was Jonah. How was he going to take all of this attention? He hadn't done so well when his father died. He didn't like people *needing* to talk to him.

She pulled into the driveway and took a deep breath. She was about to find out what he thought about it. His day couldn't have been any easier. She was sure of it.

When Melissa pushed open the front door, she was sure she'd lost her mind. She could still smell the roses. As she stepped further into the house, she realized why. There had to be another ten vases full of roses of all different colors.

Jonah walked around from the kitchen, juice bag in hand and an enormous smile on his face. "What do you think, Mom?"

"What is all this?"

"Jesse sent them."

Her mother followed Jonah out of the kitchen, wiping her hands on a towel. "They came from different florists from different towns all day. I think you made a good impression on him."

"I think he's lost his mind," Melissa retorted, knowing it wasn't a good sign, but she could feel a smile settle on her lips.

"Mom, are you going to go out with him again?" Jonah asked and took a sip from his pouch.

"I don't know. I don't think it's a good idea."

His brows drew closer. "Why? He likes you."

"He's nine years younger than me, and we don't run in the same circles."

"So."

This wasn't quite the conversation she'd expected. "Let's just say this town isn't ready for that."

Jonah nodded. "Tell me about it. Everyone knows you went out with him last night. They talked about it all day."

So he did have to deal with it. She knew it would reach him. Jonah didn't need that. "And did it bother you that they were all talking about me?"

"Why? I think you're lucky."

Melissa set her hand on her chest, which was aching. "Why am I lucky?"

"Because he likes you."

"He's famous."

"So is Mr. Carter, and no one cares anymore."

The ache began to ease. "No one thinks Mr. Carter is important?"

"That's not what I said." He blew into the juice pouch and inflated it. "It's just now they know him. He used to be a big time football guy, and now he's the football coach and a dad. Big deal. I met Jesse. He came here. I think he's a nice guy."

"You're not just saying that because you have a poster of him in your room?"

"I'm ten. I'm not dumb." He slowly flattened the pouch between his palms. "He likes you, and he makes you happy. You haven't been happy in a long time."

The ache in her chest had become a lead weight in her stomach. There she thought she'd had a grasp on life and was worried about Jonah. Who would have thought she'd been the miserable one, and Jonah had been worried about her.

"Jonah, I don't know that seeing Jesse is going to work out. I don't want you to be upset about that."

"Mom, enjoy it while it lasts. Sure, maybe you won't get married and I won't have brothers and sisters, but maybe you'll have a good time while it lasts. That can't hurt, can it?"

She could feel tears welling in her eyes, and when she looked at her mother, she was wiping tears from her eyes with the towel she hand in her hand.

Melissa walked over to her son and wrapped her arms tightly around him. "You're an amazing kid."

He wiggled, trying to get away. "I know. Can I just go over to Nathan's and play? You're too cuddly."

She laughed and released him. "Yes. One hour."

"An hour?" He darted for the back door. "Cool. See? Jesse is already working out. You only let me out for thirty minutes last week."

The door slammed behind him, and Melissa's mother laughed. "That kid is a piece of work. But he's happy for you."

"I don't see this working out, Mom."

"Then maybe you'd better get some of your son's attitude. Find a bright side for once," she said as she turned back to the kitchen.

That night Melissa carried a vase of roses to her room and set them on the nightstand. She shut her bedroom door, turned on the TV, and went into the bathroom to ready herself for bed.

As she settled into place for a quiet moment, her cell phone rang. It was ten o'clock. No one called her that late, but when she saw the caller ID come up with Jesse's name, her heart rate kicked up.

"Hello," she said quietly as to not wake up the others.

"You didn't happen to think of me today, did you?"

She chuckled and relaxed against her pillows. "You shouldn't have done that."

"I had fun."

"Well, thank you."

"I was worried about the one I sent to your school. I shouldn't have done that."

At least he had some common sense buried in those good looks, she thought. "No one knows anything."

"I missed you."

Her heart beat even harder. Why did she even care about this man? She didn't want to, but she was slipping into a territory she hadn't been in for years. There was a giddiness to her when she heard his voice. She'd gone into Jonah's room three times just to look at the poster of him. This wasn't good.

"Where are you?" she asked and then decided to retract. "Never mind. You don't have to tell me."

Jesse laughed. "I just finished a show."

"Calling me after work?"

"Yeah, I guess I am. How was your day?"

"Lots of teenagers with lots of questions about me dating you."

She heard him let out a deep breath into the phone. "I'm sorry. This can't be easy for you."

"Jonah says I should suck it up."

"I like him. Smart kid."

"He sure is."

She could hear him walking with the phone and then the background was quiet. "Listen, I know me coming into your life isn't easy. I wouldn't blame you if you told me to take a hike."

Melissa sighed. "I'd thought about it."

"Oh."

"I'm older than you. I have a normal job. I have a kid. I live in a small town full of small town gossips. But, there is something about you."

"I'm charming."

She laughed. "You are charming." She adjusted under her sheets. "I was worried most about Jonah, but he seems to be worried about me never being happy."

"I know. We talked."

She sat up in her bed. "You talked?"

"I called the house looking for you earlier, before the show. He said you hadn't gotten home yet. He's a great kid. He really looks out for you."

She'd never noticed before, but she was starting to. "He thinks you're good for me."

"I hope so. I want to be good to you, too. You deserve that."

"You don't know me."

"But I want to."

How had this all happened? Who ever thought something so crazy would happen to her. "Jesse, I don't know what I can offer you."

"I'm not looking for anything. Let's start with friendship, okay? I know this isn't normal for you, but I'm just a normal guy and I'm very attracted to you."

Again, she couldn't imagine. "I haven't been in a relationship in a very long time."

"Sure you have. You're a mother and a teacher. Those are some very important relationships."

Again, he was very wise. "You're still planning on coming for dinner on Sunday?"

"If you don't mind."

She took a deep breath. "I think I'm actually looking forward to it."

"Good. I knew I bought that truck for a reason. Well, I have to go. I have a radio interview to give. Goodnight, Melissa."

She closed her eyes and imagined his face. "Goodnight."

She turned off the phone and nestled herself into bed. As she closed her eyes, she thought of Jesse. The memory of his kiss had her pressing her lips together. Would he always make her feel so good about everything?

Melissa reached for the remote and turned off the TV. What would Martin think of such a crazy thing? Guilt began to flutter in her stomach. Martin. How could she possibly close her eyes and think of another man? Maybe this wasn't going to work out at all.

Chapter Six

William was waiting inside Melissa's classroom the next morning. It had been, in the very recent past, that when she saw him she'd be very happy to have his company. However, ever since Jesse Charles happened into her life, things had been different.

Seeing William Scott seated behind her desk only managed to make her angry.

"Morning, William. Can I help you with something?"

"Smells nice in here. You didn't take your flowers home."

She saw no reason to let him know she was well stocked in the floral department at her house. "They add a nice touch."

"Listen," he said as he stood and walked toward her. "You and I seem to be…at odds this past week. I just wanted to make sure we're okay."

"William, we are fine. It's been a little different, I'll admit. But I'm not willing to let a lifetime friendship go down the drain because you're worried."

She saw the anger flare in his eyes, but true to his nature, he let it fizzle down before he spoke. "I want you and Jonah to be happy and safe. That's all."

"I know." She touched his arm and passed by him.

"So, how about that night out? You and me? Grand Junction. Dinner. Dancing."

"I have plans this weekend," she said as she set her bag on her desk.

"Plans?"

Now his temper had moved to the vein in his temple. She hadn't seen him this mad in years. "William, do you think there is more going on between you and me than I know about?"

He swallowed hard, walked to the door, and closed it.

"I have taken care of you and Jonah for the past three years. You and I have…something, don't we?"

This was not a conversation she'd planned on having—ever. "William, you are a very dear friend. I didn't realize your feelings were more than that."

"Neither did I." His voice had softened. He ran his hand over his hair and let out a breath. "I just think that this Jesse character is messing with you. Don't get me wrong. You're a very attractive and intelligent woman…"

"But why would a famous singer want to be with me?" Now her voice sounded as pathetic as his had.

"Listen," he said as he took her hands in his. "I didn't know I had any feelings until he came along. As far as I was concerned, I thought we were doing okay, and who knows, maybe I thought it would all change someday. Martin was my best friend. When he died it was just the right thing to do, to take care of you and Jonah. But there was more there."

She knew that, but she'd denied it herself.

"William, why are you telling me this? Why now?"

She heard the bell ring, and soon the students were going to fill the halls. It would be even worse for her if they saw him holding her hands than it was for them to know she kissed Jesse Charles.

"I just don't want you to get hurt. I don't want this punk filling your head with ideas. You know what guys like him are like. They're only out for one thing."

"And if that were true, don't you suppose there would be a line of women offering it up."

He finally dropped her hands, as if he were aware of the kids in the hallway. "That's why I think this is a game to him.

Just don't let him hurt you. I may not always be here to pick up the pieces."

She felt the heat fill her cheeks. How dare he…

The door opened, and her first student walked in. William gave her a smile and turned to leave the room.

The minute the last bell of the day gave way to the freedom of the masses, Melissa gathered her bag and headed straight to William's office.

He was standing just inside when she walked in and slammed the door behind her.

"How dare you talk to me the way you did this morning. What I do in my personal life is of no business to you."

William's eyes shot open wide. He stepped to the side just the slightest bit to acknowledge the woman seated in the chair behind him.

He swallowed hard. "Mrs. Mathews, I'd like to introduce you to Mrs. Zucker." He turned back to her, his lips pursed. "She's trying to decide between Aspen Creek or Aspen Hills for her son's scholastic needs when they move here in the spring."

Melissa was sure embarrassment wouldn't kill her, but at that moment, it felt as though it were choking the life out of her.

She forced a smile to her face. "Mrs. Zucker, it is a pleasure to meet you. I grew up in Aspen Creek with my late husband and Mr. Scott here." She figured if the woman understood that they'd known each other since they were children, her outburst wouldn't seem so crazy. "My own son attends the middle school. So I assure you, sans my bad morning, Aspen Creek boasts the finest schools."

The woman, with an equally forced smile, nodded.

William excused them and stepped through the door with Melissa into the main office.

"I assume you have more to say to me," he growled, keeping his voice quiet.

"I'm sorry. Please let Mrs. Zucker know I'm not crazy and that I apologize to her as well."

He nodded and walked back to his office. He gave her one more displeased look before he shut the door between them.

Who would have thought that having known the principal since he was ten was not a comfort when, even in her thirties, it still scared the hell out of her when his eyes became focused and his jaw jutted out.

Melissa took a drive the long way around town before she crossed Rose Bridge. She passed her street and headed up the mountain.

The road grew narrow and the trees thicker as she climbed higher. The town below her looked calm through the aspen groves.

Ahead of her she could see the gate which would welcome her to her grandfather's land. It was a short, twenty minute drive from town, yet as she looked through the trees she could still see the small town nestled in the valley below her.

High above her grandfather's land, she could see the glimmer from the front gate of the Rose estate. Why did it seem so strange to her that Jesse Charles had visited the town when she herself had been friends with the great-granddaughter of the late Lilly Rose.

Melissa smiled as she drove through the open gate toward her grandfather's house.

Lilly Rose had been a golden screen icon. She'd been in love with one man, an older man, and married to some Hollywood director. Yet her roots were there, right where Melissa's were, in Aspen Creek.

She parked her car in front of the house. It was dark and deserted, which was something she didn't like. Her grandfather had been moved to a nursing home. Her grandmother had passed away years before. Now the old ranch was for sale, and she wished she could buy it and live there with her mother and Jonah. But on her mother's fixed income and her teacher's salary, they struggled just to pay the taxes on the land.

The weather vane on the roof of the barn glimmered when the sun hit it just right. There was a time when she'd sit on the porch and watch it spin in the wind.

Melissa stepped out of her car just as she heard a car drive up the dirt road from the gate. It was no surprise when William's car was headed toward her.

He was quick to jump out of his car and head right for her, but his anger seemed to defuse the closer he got.

"She wasn't sold on the sanity of my staff."

Melissa nodded, unsure if he was serious or joking with her. "I'm so sorry..."

"What has gotten into you?" He stepped closer. "I've never seen you so hot and cold." His words carried on the cold air.

"I'm just a bit out of sorts."

"And this Jesse Charles crap is making it worse."

She turned toward the house and started up the front step when he reached for her arm and turned her around.

"I'm sorry. You deserve to have someone give you attention like that. I just don't think it should be him."

"And you had someone more deserving in mind?"

William stepped up onto the same rickety step and looked down at her. He touched her face with his soft leather gloved hand. "I know it's the wrong time to tell you that I've had feelings for you since we were fifteen."

"I wouldn't believe you anyway."

He laughed. "I wasn't very nice for a few years."

"You could say that again." She turned and took the next step, but he again reached for her, this time taking hold of her hand.

"Listen, I know this Jesse Charles thing is something you need to feel out, but he's going to hurt you."

"You don't know that."

"I can feel it." He let out a deep breath into the cold. "I'll be here. I'll always be here."

"I never doubted that."

William shook his head. "I mean, God forbid, if he breaks your heart, I want to be the one to pick up the pieces. I'd be a good father to Jonah, and I'd do everything to be a decent husband to you."

Melissa dropped her shoulders. He'd accused her of having had something get into her, and perhaps she was the crazy one, but was William Scott actually standing before her professing his love to her?

"William, stop." She took another step and then turned to him. "I can't even believe you're saying all of this. One, I don't know why you're saying it at all. Two, why now? Why wait until someone else is interested."

"Because I'm scared."

"Of what?"

"Of you getting hurt."

Melissa turned again and walked toward the door. William followed and the porch creaked under him. "Watch that board. It's loose."

He looked down. "On the first warm day I'll come fix it."

"I'm sure it'll be sold by then." Her voice dropped as she pushed open the door. "That'll be a very sad day."

Melissa stepped inside, and William closed the door behind him. "You know, I have enough saved that we could secure the house and the land."

"Why would you do that for us?"

"Melissa…"

"Don't say anymore." She held up a hand to him. "I'm still processing everything else you've said."

"I didn't say it to upset you."

She felt it brewing inside of her, the heat of anger. "Well, it did upset me. You don't seem to think I'm worthy of having Jesse Charles, or anyone else, be interested in me. Well, why not? I have a lot to offer. Why couldn't some sexy, young man want me? I mean, well, he could."

"All I'm saying is…"

"All you're saying is that now that someone has shown intent, you're the boss over my whole life. Well, that's not the case. Thank you for stepping up when Martin died, but no one asked you to. Jonah and I would be fine without you."

She wasn't sure it was what she'd meant, but she'd said it and it had hurt him nearly as bad to hear it as it had hurt her to say it.

He tucked his hands into the pockets of his coat. "I understand. I didn't mean any harm." He turned to the door and then back to Melissa. "I'll wait and drive down behind you, if you'd like. The pass is slick."

"I've been driving it for years, William. I will be fine."

He nodded slowly and left.

Melissa stood in the dusty living room among the covered furniture and watched as William drove away in his car. Her heart ached for him. What had he been thinking? Why did his opinion bother her so badly?

Her cell phone rang in her pocket. She pulled it out and answered it sharply, "Hello."

"Hello, beautiful." Jesse's voice was soft on the other end. "I hope I didn't catch you at a bad time. I was heading out to the bus and thought I'd try to catch you before you were sitting down to dinner."

Melissa let the tension in her shoulders roll away. "I was just checking on my grandpa's house before I headed home."

"The house on the hill?"

She smiled at the memory of the night she told him that. "Yes."

"You know, I was watching TV last night after I hung up with you, and an old Lilly Rose movie was on. I was thinking about her house by your grandpa's."

"She was a real beauty."

He laughed softly. "Are you sure you're not related to her? I think you look a lot alike. You have that natural glamour beauty to you too."

She couldn't help but let words like that affect her. He delivered them so flawlessly. But what if William was right? What if Jesse Charles just wanted something from her?

"Melissa, are you still there?"

"Yes," she said, realizing she'd been standing in the quiet house dwelling on things that weren't real. "And thank you. I guess it's been a long time since someone has complimented me like that. I forgot how to react." She moved about the lower portion of the house making sure everything was in order.

"Listen, I have to go, but the reason I called was I'll be flying into Grand Junction much earlier than I'd first planned. I know we discussed dinner on Sunday, but you wouldn't be up for breakfast and lunch too, would you?"

She laughed as she started her climb of the stairs, which creaked under her feet. "I have to be in church Sunday morning. But you're welcome to come."

"Church? Wow, it's been a long time since…"

"If you're uncomfortable…"

"What I was going to say was it's just been a long time since I've been in a church. I think some praise is in order. What time?"

She had to clear her head as she opened the door to her grandparents' bedroom and gazed over the old furniture her grandfather had built and her grandmother had stained. "Ten."

"I'll be there in plenty of time."

There was a peace in making plans with him even though she was sure that Sunday would be the last day she'd ever see him. "I'll see you then."

"Can I call you tomorrow?"

Oh, he was cute. "Yes, I think I'd like that."

"I know I would."

They said their goodbyes, and Melissa tucked her phone back into her pocket as she closed the door to the bedroom. For a moment she stood there thinking about Jesse and how his voice and words had soothed her nerves after William had stirred her up.

This was what happened to women and famous musicians. They were good with words and the delivery was part of the charm. Was she falling for Jesse Charles's flattery? Or was there really some merit to how he felt about her?

She looked down at her finger where her wedding ring still remained on her finger.

No matter what happened, there were two men who seemed to be interested in her, for whatever reason. The only thing that was clear—it was time to move on.

Melissa walked back through the house and out the front door, missing the rotting board by the door.

She drove down the road to the entrance, got out of her car, and secured the gate. As she began her decent back toward town, the static on the radio gave way to the music.

Any other time she'd have turned off the radio, but this time it was Jesse's voice she heard and he was singing *Admirer*—only this time it was as if he were singing to her.

As she rounded the base of the mountain, she noticed that the palms of her hands were hot and her heart beat was quickened.

Dear Lord, this was more than admiration for a man she'd only met. This wasn't even a crush, like so many of the girls had on him.

In only a few meetings and phone calls, she was having feelings for a younger man whom the whole world was watching. If she wasn't careful she'd fall in love with him, but was that what she wanted?

She drove down her street and looked at all the houses that lined it. Houses filled with families.

Could Jesse Charles offer her that? William Scott could.

She pulled into her driveway and put the car in park.

She was falling in love with Jesse, but in reality, it was William who could give her the stability that Jonah needed.

She covered her face with her hands and sat there. By the end of Sunday she would know. She'd know Jesse's intentions. She'd better understand her options and how she felt about them.

There was no denying she'd rather have her husband back. But Jesse Charles had been removing him from her mind. Was that a blessing or a curse?

Deep down inside, she sure would like to find out.

Chapter Seven

It hadn't gone unnoticed that William hadn't talked to Melissa almost all week. There had been a few work related necessities, but that was it.

Before Jesse Charles, she'd have been devastated, but as she wiped down the kitchen at nearly eleven o'clock on Saturday night, she knew it was a good thing. She was nervous enough knowing Jesse was going to be there in a few hours. How bad would she have been if William had more time to make her crazy?

But it was getting late, and she needed to get to bed and stop worrying about either one of them.

She turned off the kitchen light just as her cell phone buzzed in her pocket.

It was a text from Jesse.

Will be there sooner than thought. Taking off now. Will be in town about 1am. Is that ok?

Was that okay? Dear Lord, she'd been nervous enough, but now he was going to come by at one in the morning? This was crazy, absolutely absurd. What was she doing? It wasn't worth what everyone in town would say—or think. No, it wasn't okay. He needed to wait. Oh, heck, he needed not to come.

But as she placed her thumbs on the keyboard of her iPhone she typed *Yes. I can't wait.* And, without thinking, she knew that was the truth.

Who cared what the world thought. Jesse Charles liked her and wanted to be with her—enough so that he was buying trucks and flying private planes to get to her.

A fluttering in her stomach had her sitting down at the kitchen table. It was real, wasn't it? A man once voted the sexiest man of the year was on his way, in the middle of the night, to spend a few extra hours with her.

She swallowed hard and then dashed off down the hall to her room to get ready.

The realization that she wasn't even going to get any sleep hit her about the time she began to freshen up her makeup and fix her hair. It was going on midnight. What was she doing?

But she didn't stop. She changed her clothes, spritzed on some perfume, and headed back to the kitchen to make a pot of coffee.

When she finally sat down on the couch with a mug of coffee in hand, she looked around. She'd been cleaning for a week. There was nothing left to do. Besides, he'd been to her house before, unexpectedly, so really she needn't worry about it.

As twelve-thirty approached and her coffee grew cold, she felt the heaviness of her eyelids. A moment of sleep wouldn't hurt anything.

A moment was nearly an hour when she sat up as soon as she'd heard a car door shut out front.

She jumped to her feet, set the mug on the coffee table, and hurried to the door.

She peered through the window at the door. He'd come. He'd really made the trip in the middle of the night, down the mountain, just to see her. It was then she noticed he was completely alone.

Trust. He trusted her. He hadn't brought a bodyguard or his manager or his assistant. This was just going to be her and Jesse.

The thought of this man wanting to be with her took over, and she flung open the door.

The bright, perfect smile on Jesse's mouth flashed even in the darkness.

He looked different. His hair wasn't spiked up, his jeans were casual, and he had on a heavy coat.

There were no words between them as she stepped out in the cold night air and met him on the porch. His hands went to her face, hers to his chest, and their lips met in a heated kiss that said each of them had been waiting for that moment.

She shivered against him, and he pulled her in tighter.

"I didn't expect you to be standing at the door," he said as he gazed down at her.

"I couldn't help it. I'd meant to tell you not to come, but…"

"I'm glad you didn't." He bent down and kissed her softly again. "Let's go inside. You're freezing."

She let her hand fall until she found his and interlaced their fingers. Then she opened the front door and led him inside.

She shut the front door quietly behind them as Jesse shrugged out of his coat.

She reached for the coat. "I'll take that."

He handed it to her, and she looked it over.

"Allstate Arena staff?" She looked back up at him, and he grinned.

"It's really cold in Chicago, and I didn't have a good coat. Then a guy heard that I was coming here and said I was crazy to fly into Grand Junction because you guys were going to get a storm coming your way. So a nice man named Ted let me have the coat."

"Is it Ted's coat?"

"No, it's officially stolen property now."

She laughed aloud and then covered her mouth, realizing that everyone else was still asleep. "You are trouble for me, aren't you?"

Jesse moved in closer to her and gathered her in his arms. "I don't mean to be. I don't want to be."

Her breath grew thick. "We come from two different worlds."

"We sure do. I like yours."

Melissa narrowed her eyes. "I have nothing."

"Oh, you have more than you think." He brushed a strand of hair from her face. "You have a family, a community, friends, and a very important job. I admire you for all of that."

"Why me? Why…"

"Shhh." He moved in closer and laid a kiss on her lips.

The coat between them kept them at a short distance, but it wasn't enough to keep the heat of his body from making her temperature rise.

Jesse pulled back and gazed at her. "You're old fashioned, aren't you?"

She didn't like how that sounded since they were so many years apart in age. "What does that mean?"

"It means you're the kind of girl who plays by rules. You meet. You date. You become boyfriend and girlfriend. A man should get down on a knee and propose with a ring, but only after getting permission to do so from her family. No babies until there is a marriage—not a wedding—but a marriage." He stood back and looked her over. "Yeah, and you go to church and Jonah told me you're a stickler for having homework done before dinner."

Melissa pursed her lips. "I sound like a fuddy duddy."

"Not in the least." He lifted his head and inhaled. "Do I smell coffee?"

"Yes. It was the only way I could keep awake. Would you like some?"

"I'd love it. And then I can tell you why I think your way of mothering is so amazing."

She nodded and headed toward the kitchen with Jesse in tow. She draped the large "borrowed" jacket over the back of a chair and then pulled a mug out of the cabinet.

Melissa poured the coffee into the mug. "So you're looking for a mother figure?"

"I knew that sounded wrong. No. But looking at it in a backward way...a good mother is a good listener and caregiver...which means she'd be an attentive wife. In turn, she must be one hell of a lover."

Melissa swallowed hard as she replaced the coffeepot back on the burner. "You've given this a lot of thought."

"Maybe not as much as you think." She handed him the mug, and he took a long, deep smell. "This smells great. Thanks."

"Sure." She refilled her empty mug that sat on the counter and then sat down across from him at the kitchen table. "I'm not some jet set beauty."

"You're more."

"I'm not a one night stand."

"I'd never think that of you."

Melissa dropped her shoulders. "So tell me, why me?"

Jesse pushed his coffee aside and reached for her hands. "Do you believe in love at first sight?"

"No," she answered quickly. She didn't want him to think that he could just move this little rendezvous along at his usual pace. And there was no way in hell she was going to let him know she'd given him more thought than she should have in the past few weeks. Hadn't she even considered that she'd fallen in love with him? How absurd.

"I do."

"You're in love with me?"

He smiled softly. "My heart aches when I can't hear your voice. My nerves get shaky when I think you assume I'm stalking you."

She laughed and he continued, "When I look at that picture of us and Jonah, I feel like I'm at home. I won't say I'm in love with you because that would make you very uncomfortable."

There he was again with his perfect words, but she listened.

"Let's just say, Melissa, I can't stop thinking about you, and I want to spend all my time with you."

She bit down on her lip. "I've been thinking about you a lot, too."

"Oh, I hoped you'd say that."

"I don't want to be thinking of you. You don't live in this world that I do."

Jesse moved his chair around to be next to her. "I want to." He picked up his mug and sipped from it again. "Let me tell you why this is all so appealing."

He touched her cheek again and simply gazed into her eyes. This was too comfortable, but she didn't want to move. There was a reason he'd been voted the sexiest man, and it was captivating to stare back into his grey eyes.

"Just because my face is on a poster in your son's room doesn't mean I chose that. I mean, I'm good at what I do. I've been built to be good at it. But I've always wanted normal."

"You mean a day-to-day job, weekly pay check, laundry, dishes, carpools…"

"Yes."

She watched him, and his mannerism didn't change as though he were feeding her a line. This was what the man wanted, and she exuded it. Was that a good thing?

"Laundry is overrated."

Jesse laughed and sat back in his chair. "Tell me about your husband."

"You sure have strange topics for a date."

"Are we on a date?" He leaned back in. "Let's go make out on the couch then."

She slapped his shoulder, and he eased back with a grin.

"Martin was a police officer. In a town like this, the force is small, but there were five of them and they got their share of action with Aspen Hills and the wayward party-goer. There have been a few petty thefts, speeders, drunks…" She let out a long breath. "He loved his job."

"You were together a long time?"

"High school."

"Wow," he said on a breath. "Hard shoes to fill."

"No one ever will." She needed to make that clear. Martin was the love of her life. Not even Jesse Charles could take that away.

"How did he die?"

She couldn't just sit and discuss it. Melissa stood and walked to the sink with her mug. She rinsed it out and stared out into the blackness beyond her kitchen window.

"Routine traffic stop. Car was coming down the mountain too fast. Martin stopped them. He had to run a plate, so he did. The car was stolen."

She took a deep breath, and her fingers curled around the edge of the counter as she continued to stare out the window.

"When he got out of the car to approach the driver, the driver pulled a gun on him and shot him in the chest."

"Oh, Melissa." Jesse stood and crossed to her. "I'm so sorry."

She shook her head. "He died on the side of the road." Tears filled her eyes, and she hurried to brush them away. "Jonah and I were in Aspen Hills for a Boy Scout function. We came over the hill only twenty minutes after they had cleared the scene."

Jesse pulled her into his arms and held her close. "Melissa, I had no idea."

"William was waiting for me when I got home. He told me what had happened. I was a mess."

"Who is William?" There was tension in his voice.

"William is Martin's best friend and my boss. He's taken very good care of us for the past three years."

The hug began to strain, and she understood why. Jesse was feeling out of place, but now she desperately wanted him there. It felt good to cry out her pain and be held by arms that offered compassion.

Melissa pulled back and looked up at him. "Some date, huh?"

He chuckled. "I didn't mean to…"

She shook her head again. "It's part of my life and Jonah's. It comes with us."

"As it should."

She stepped back and dropped her shoulders. "Should we just go out to the couch and make out?"

"Sounds like a lot more fun."

Melissa moved in against him again. "I can't figure out how to act around you."

He smoothed his hand over her hair. "Natural."

"You bring something out in me that I didn't know existed."

"Are you happy?"

She thought for a moment and then rested her head against his chest. "I've been very happy this week. Enough so that I realized I wasn't happy before."

"Then that makes me happy." He kissed the top of her head. "Now, can we go do that making out thing?"

Jesse laughed and wrapped his arm around her shoulders as she led him to the living room, all the while wondering how she was going to make him go away forever—because that was what needed to happen, even if her heart wasn't in it.

Chapter Eight

Though there were plenty more kisses as they curled themselves around each other on the couch, there wasn't any more than that. Both of them were exhausted. Jesse hadn't wanted to watch regular TV. He said there was just too much junk on TV. Melissa thought a musical was in order.

She flipped through her DVDs. "*The Sound of Music?*"

Jesse shrugged. "I've never seen it."

Melissa nearly dropped the book of DVDs. "Are you kidding me? Who hasn't seen this?" She held the disk out in front of her.

"Me."

"Julie Andrews? Christopher Plumber?"

He laughed. "I know the people in it, and I know all the songs. I've just never sat down and watched it."

"Well, if you want to be with me, you'd better see it."

"Then hurry and put it in."

His eyes were playful, but soft. She took the cue and inserted the disk into the player, retrieved the remote, and sat back down next to him. He pulled her in closer to him, and she started the movie.

Melissa remembered the family beginning to flee after the concert, but the next thing she heard was her own mother's voice.

It was then she realized that she'd fallen asleep on the couch, wrapped under a blanket with Jesse's arm wrapped around her.

The DVD repeated the menu items, and the music played over and over as she tried to comprehend the moment.

"Missy, get up. Pastor is expecting you early for sermon," her mother said, standing over her.

"Oh, no." The realization finally hit her, and she jarred upright.

Jesse sprang upright as well.

"Hurry, I have to go." Melissa kicked away the blanket and ran down the hall.

Jesse pried his eyes open and then looked at Patsy and Jonah, who both stood there smiling at him.

He tried to gather his wits and stand up. "I'm sorry about this." He motioned to the couch.

"I didn't even know you'd come." Patsy gathered the blanket from the couch and proceeded to fold it.

"I got in very early this morning. She said it was okay to come over." He noticed Jonah standing behind Patsy, smiling. "How are you this morning, Jonah?"

"Good. Are you going to church with us?"

He'd nearly forgotten. "Oh, yeah. I packed some nicer clothes. They're in the truck."

"I'll go get 'em." Jonah moved past his grandmother.

Jesse laughed as he pulled the keys from his pocket. "Blue bag in the passenger seat."

Jonah nodded and headed out the door.

Patsy set the quilt on the chair behind her. "You look exhausted."

"It's been a long night."

"You guys could have gotten a better night's sleep in a bed."

He swallowed hard. "I don't think that was an option."

Patsy smiled and gave him a nod. "She's old fashioned, that one."

He chuckled. "I told her that, too."

"She's not going to go for any funny business. She's got Jonah, you know."

This was more like it, he thought. Some motherly concern. The world was in short supply of such things.

"I understand. I have some very strong feelings for your daughter."

Patsy winked. "I know. And she'll come around."

Jonah walked back through the door with the bag and handed it to him.

Patsy looked at her watch. "We have to drive away in a half hour."

"I'll hurry."

"You can use the bathroom down the hall."

"Thanks." He started down the hallway.

"Oh, and Jesse…" He turned around to see Patsy walk toward the kitchen. "I'm glad to have you here."

The morning was rushed in the little household, and he enjoyed it. Melissa had run past him as she came out of the bedroom and raced to the kitchen. She poured a cup of coffee and quickly threw two pieces of bread into the toaster.

She took down a second mug and poured him coffee, too.

"I'm sorry for the rush. Do you like jelly on your toast?"

He couldn't help but smile at her. This side of her was maybe even more endearing than seeing her in the frog vest.

"That would be super. Can I help you with anything?"

She turned and narrowed her eyes at him, but shook her head as if he'd asked an unanswerable question.

"Jonah, it's snowing out. Make sure you get your coat."

"Got it, Mom." Jonah hollered from the other room.

"And don't forget your workbook. Mrs. Pete says she wants to look at them this week."

"Got it, Mom. Let's just go."

The bread popped out of the top of toaster, and only a moment later, Jesse was handed a warm piece of jellied bread.

He was sure it was not normal to be almost giddy about the crazy pace and the meager carbohydrate breakfast he was about to consume as they ran out of the house for church, but if he could, he'd have jumped up and down with excitement. This was exactly what he was trying to tell her about. This was the life.

Jonah and Patsy opened the back doors, but Jesse made it to the car quicker to stop Melissa's mother from sitting in the back seat. "You should be in front. I'll sit back here with Jonah."

"That's mighty kind of you."

Jesse opened the passenger door, and Patsy slid past him. Melissa stood on the other side of the car, and a smile formed on her lips. Then quietly she mouthed the words *thank you.*

Jesse shut the door and climbed in back with Jonah.

"Have you ever been to church?" he asked.

"It has been a very long time."

"We go every Sunday. Are you going to go with us next week, too?"

Jesse had never been around kids. Usually they were awkward around him, especially ten-year-olds.

"We'll have to see what my schedule is like."

Jonah nodded as though that was good enough for him. Now if only he could get his manager to accept answers like that.

"Where did you have a concert last night?"

"Chicago."

"Where is that?"

Jesse smiled. "Illinois."

Jonah wrinkled up his nose. "And you're already here?"

"Yep."

Jonah crossed his arms over his chest. "Where did you wake up yesterday morning?"

"In Los Angeles."

"And then you worked in Chicago?"

"Yep."

"And you spent the night in Colorado?"

Jesse laughed. "Yes."

"That is so cool. I've only been to Idaho three times. You were in three states in one day."

He kept the smile on his lips, but when he looked up at Melissa, he could see her questioning look in the mirror. His life certainly didn't fit with hers, did it?

"Where do you go next?" Jonah asked.

Jesse had to think. "I think Saint Louis."

Jonah thought for a moment. "Missouri?"

"Yeah."

"Cool."

Melissa pulled into the parking lot of the church. Cars filtered in from all directions. He had to remind himself this was a small town. This is what they did on Sunday mornings. He, on the other hand, used Sunday mornings—if he was home—to recuperate from traveling. He had a lot to be thankful for. Perhaps a morning in church was overdue.

As soon as the car was parked, Jesse hurried out of the car and opened Patsy's door. He held out his hand to help her out.

"Thank you," she said, smiling up at him.

Melissa again gave him what he would call an untrusting look, but then her door opened.

"Can I help you out, Mom?"

Jesse smiled. Jonah was following suit. Well, maybe he'd done some good with his visit.

Melissa looked at him and then back at Jonah, who also held out his hand to help her out.

"Thank you," she said and her voice quivered.

"You're welcome, Mom."

Patsy bunched her coat around her with her hands and headed toward the door. "Missy, you'd better get in there. Pastor is going to have a fit if you're not there before the congregation."

"I'm hurrying," she called from the car as she gathered her purse and shut the door behind her.

She hurried up to them. "Will you be okay with Mom?"

"You're not sitting with us?"

"No." She hurried ahead of them and into the church.

Jesse thought stage fright was bad, but this had hit a new level.

Patsy laced her arm through his. "You'll be just fine with us."

She lifted her head and walked through the doors of the church.

Jesse humored to himself that all churches smelled the same. It was familiar to him, and that seemed odd.

But then the familiar sounds penetrated his ears. It wasn't sounds of the congregation gathering, it was whispers. They knew who he was, and they knew he was on the arm of the biology teacher's mother's arm. He swallowed hard. It had been a long time since he'd been this uncomfortable.

Patsy walked toward the sanctuary, and the pastor stood at the door.

"Oh, Patsy Bartlett, how are you this find morning?" he asked.

"I'm cold," she laughed. "Pastor, I'd like to introduce you to our guest. This is Mr. Charles."

The pastor shook his hand. "Mr. Charles, it is a pleasure to meet you."

"Likewise, sir."

"You are a singer, correct?"

Jesse's stomach tightened as his nerves took over. "Yes."

"Well, it is wonderful to have you." He looked down at Jonah. "I saw your mother as she ran in this morning. She said you did wonderful on your spelling test."

Jonah smiled wide. "I got an A plus."

"That is wonderful." The pastor shifted his eyes back to Patsy. "Thank you for coming this morning and bringing your friend." He gave Jesse a nod. "We will see you after the sermon."

Patsy nodded and, still on Jesse's arm, she walked into the sanctuary.

Heads turned as they walked down the center aisle. Why was this so uncomfortable? Jesse was used to having eyes on him at all times. Even the occasional paparazzi fell out of trees trying to get pictures of him, but having Melissa's community whisper among themselves and keep a steady eye on him made him very nervous—not for himself, but for Melissa. This was so unfair to her. Why had he come?

Patsy found a pew, and she ushered Jonah in first. She followed, and Jesse followed her.

He leaned in toward her. "Where is Melissa?"

"You'll see her soon," she said, folding her hands in her lap as the pastor headed toward the podium and the choir began to filter in.

A man walked up next to them in the aisle. Jonah immediately scooted down, as did Patsy, so Jesse followed their lead.

"Jesse," Patsy whispered. "This is William Scott. William, this is Jesse."

Jesse shook the man's hand and remembered that this was the man Melissa had mentioned. Her late husband's best friend and her boss.

William's grip was tight, but Jesse was used to that. People were usually intimidated by him, so they thought an overly firm handshake would make them superior.

"So, you're the rock star?"

Oh, the man already hated him. "I'm a musician. Yes."

William gave a low hum and turned his attention to the altar.

At the end of the line of choir members was Melissa in a purple robe with a white collar. There was probably some sin in thinking that was sexy, but he couldn't help himself.

The choir took their positions, but Melissa walked past them and took her position just to the side of the altar between the choir and the pastor.

The pastor opened his Bible and looked out at the congregation. He then proceeded to begin his sermon, and as he did, Melissa's hands lifted and she signed every word the pastor spoke.

Jesse felt his breath catch in his chest. It was beautiful— almost dance-like. He couldn't take his eyes off of her.

The fluid motion of her fingers and hands carried the words of the sermon and the choir to someone in the congregation, but, for him, it embedded her deeper into his heart.

This woman he was falling in love with was full of many, many surprises.

Melissa had noticed that Jesse had never once taken his eyes off her.

In her life, she had been nervous to interpret a service, but today—this was different.

"Melissa, you did beautifully today," Mrs. Johnson said, touching her arm as she passed by.

"Thank you."

"Your grandfather would be proud."

Melissa hung up her robe as Emmy hurried up to her. "He came to church with you?" She grabbed Melissa's arm and jumped up and down. "I can't believe this. I didn't know this was a serious thing."

Melissa grabbed hold of her to stop her. "It's not. He just came to visit."

"That's twice!"

"Shhh." Melissa looked around, and eyes were on her from every direction. "This is the last time. Look how this makes everyone."

"So? I think this is wonderful."

"Because he's Jesse Charles?"

Emmy tilted her head. "Because he likes you." She considered Melissa for a moment. "You're stuck on his fame, aren't you? And I don't mean that in a good way."

"This isn't good for Jonah."

"I think Jonah is handling it better than you."

As Emmy walked away, Melissa thought about that. She was right. She certainly wasn't handling it well at all.

She started out of the church when the pastor caught her at the door.

"You did a beautiful job as always, Melissa."

"Thank you."

"I met your guest." He held his Bible to his chest and crossed his arms over it. "I didn't know you liked his kind of music."

"Well, Sir, I don't. But we have become friends, and his music doesn't play into that."

"Friends?"

"Yes. Only friends."

The pastor nodded. "How is this affecting Jonah?"

It was just proof that she was right. This was so very wrong on so many levels. And worse, everyone on her street would know he'd been there all night. What they wouldn't know was she was sitting on the couch with him, watching musicals.

"Jonah adores him."

"I'd hate to see him get hurt. He's only now moving on from his father's tragedy."

She was well aware of that. This wasn't a conversation she wanted to be having. "He's fine."

"Well, then I'll see you next week. Thank you for signing for Mr. and Mrs. Dupree. They appreciate it."

"Always my pleasure."

Melissa walked out to the parking lot. Her mother was surrounded by many of her usual friends, but the difference was she had Jesse still on her arm.

The only reason Melissa wanted to laugh was the horrified look on Jesse's face. But she knew her mother was protecting him.

She could hear the whispers, and she'd seen that every other set of eyes in the church had been on Jesse during the sermon. Perhaps that's why the pastor seemed so unimpressed with her guest.

Even as she walked toward Jesse, she could see the small groups of students huddling around. She was sure if her mother hadn't had him on her arm, they'd have all pounced on him to get an autograph.

It was then she noticed Jonah stood guard on his other side. They were a compassioned pair, and they really seemed to like Jesse—and not because he was a pop star.

"Melissa, you did beautifully," one lady said as she approached.

"Your grandfather must be so proud of you," another added.

Mrs. Hart took hold of her hand. "We've been talking with your new boyfriend. He's quite a nice young man."

Melissa looked at Jesse, whose eyes had opened wide.

"C'mon, let's head home," Patsy said to defuse the group as the air began to stir and the bitter chill of a pending storm began to blow through.

Just as Jesse opened the car door for Melissa, she heard her name called across the lot. William hurried toward her as the snow began to softly fall from the sky.

"You were beautiful today," he said.

"Thank you. William have you met…"

"Yes," he curtly said and gave Jesse a glance.

Jesse touched her hand. "I'll let you two talk." He gave William a nod and walked around the car and climbed inside with her mother and Jonah.

Melissa closed her car door.

"What are you doing?" William asked, his tone hushed.

"I'm going home. I'm freezing out here."

"That's not what I mean. I heard he spent the night."

God, the gossips in this town were fast. "He came in in the middle of the night. That's when his plane got in."

"He's staying with you?"

"For the day." She looked around the lot as it emptied out, and the snow began to fall faster. "Really, William, he's just here to visit."

"Melissa, is this what you want? The whole town is talking about you."

"Well, then, they'd better get used to him being here."

William moved in closer to her and held her arms in his hands. "This is what you want? I offer you stability, and you choose to be the town gossip?"

"It's my life. Butt out."

"I would, but Martin always told me to look out for you. I'm doing what he asked me to do."

Anger burned inside of her. "This isn't fair. I'm going home with this man, and if he chooses to stay the night then so be it. It's no one's business but my own."

She reached for the door, and he took hold of her hand. She could see Jesse in the car move as if he were thinking that she needed protection.

"If the town talks, they might not hurt you. But think about Jonah. You're hurting Jonah."

He let go of her hand and walked away toward his car.

Melissa opened the door and climbed in. Damn it, he was right. Already rumors were running, and her students were harder to get through to. Now she had to deal with the fact that the consequences to Jonah were going to be worse.

She started the car and batted back the angry tears that were forming.

The worst part was she was starting to have feelings for Jesse that she hadn't had in a very long time. She wasn't sure she was ready to let that go.

Chapter Nine

The ride back to their house was quiet. Jesse knew that whatever William had said to her had upset her deeply. The man didn't like him. He'd gotten that vibe loud and clear as they were seated next to each other at church. But Jesse was sure things between William and Melissa were more serious than she let on. He was certainly in the way.

The only problem was that he didn't want to let go.

As they drove into the driveway, Patsy turned in her seat to look at him. "You're staying for lunch, right?"

He glanced at Melissa, who nodded in the mirror.

"I would love to."

"Great." Patsy turned to Jonah. "Come inside with me and help me get lunch started." She turned to Melissa. "Maybe you two should take a drive and have some time. You should go show Jesse Grandpa's land. You can unlock the gate while you're there. Elsie is going to show it tomorrow."

Melissa opened her mouth to speak, but Patsy hurried out of the car and Jonah retreated quickly, too. Jesse opened the door, climbed out of the car, and then got back into the front seat.

"Melissa, if you don't want to…"

She shook her head. "I do want to." She lifted her head and her eyes were filled with tears. "Jesse, this isn't going to work. How can we possibly make this work?"

He touched her cheek. He was good with words to soothe her, but he knew this was nearly the end of them and they hadn't even begun. She'd been right. They just came from two different worlds.

"We have today. Be mine for today. We can figure out everything later."

She nodded, put the car in reverse, and headed up the mountain as the snow began to come down heavier.

"Where did you learn to sign like that?" Jesse asked as Melissa maneuvered the narrowing road.

"My grandfather is deaf."

"The grandfather whose house we're going to now?" Panic took over.

"He's not there."

"Oh, that's right."

She smiled. "He liked his house, buried in the mountains. The community accepted him, but in general, the deaf were not commonly accepted by the masses. But up here, it didn't matter."

Jesse looked between the trees and down the mountain. The small, quaint town began to grow smaller as they climbed the narrow, steep road.

"So this was his hideaway?"

"You could say that. He and Grandma lived here for fifty years together. When he lost her, we lost a little of him. We had to put him in a home in Aspen Hills. But he's doing well there. I just wish we could put him somewhere even better."

"What's stopping you?"

She quickly glanced at him and then back to the road, which was quickly filling with snow.

"We live on my teaching income and my mother's Social Security. There is no money to put him somewhere nicer. The only option for us is to sell his property."

Just as she said so, they reached the property line with its grand ornate gate at the entrance.

Melissa stopped the car, took out the keys, and opened the car door. "I have to unlock the gate. I'll be right back."

He watched as she shielded her eyes from the blowing snow and unlocked the gate. The snow had accumulated quickly, and she had to force the gate open enough for her car to pass through.

Snow storms, narrow mountain roads, manual entry gates—what a different world. How wondrous, he thought.

When she opened the car door, the gust of cold air chilled him to the bone. As she situated in her seat, engulfed in her heavier coat, he couldn't help but smile at the bright red of her cheeks.

Melissa pulled through the gate and toward the house.

"You should keep my truck and use it. How do you drive in the snow in this car?"

She chuckled. "Skill and finance. I own this outright and that makes a big difference."

God, how spoiled was he? Within ten minutes, he'd heard twice how hard things were for her, and here he was in a stolen coat, bragging about a truck he bought on a whim after flying into town on a private plane. When did he become what he loathed?

Melissa parked the car in front of the house. Jesse cranked his neck to see it through the window.

"This is awesome."

She laughed. "It is, isn't it? My great grandfather started the house, and my grandfather added a room in the back to it. A laundry room of all things." She turned her head. "The barn was my playhouse. Grandpa even made me a little escape up on the second level." She sighed. "I miss that simplicity."

She adjusted the zipper on her coat. "Out back there is a tiny little retention pond with a rope swing. You can swing and dive in. Jonah likes that the best."

"You glow when you talk about this place."

"I glow?" She touched her cheeks. "Well, it holds many good memories. I'll miss it when it's gone."

Obviously she was done talking about it because she opened her door, climbed out of the car, and shut the door behind her.

Jesse climbed out of the car into the cold wind and followed her up the steps to the large front porch.

"Watch this board by the door. It's rotted through."

He stepped to the side. Getting hurt the night before a concert was not a good idea.

When she pushed open the door, he was transported to another time. The wood floors were raw, unfinished, unmatched pieces of wood. The furniture was old and most of it was covered.

The air was thick with dust, but it didn't bother him at all.

"This place is amazing."

"It's not as big as it looks from outside. This is the living room." She turned to the small space behind them. "That's the dining room, and the kitchen is through there. The laundry room is just off the back. It doubles as a closed porch and a mud room."

"There are bedrooms upstairs?"

"Three."

He felt the smile form on his face. "Can I see them?"

"Of course."

She led him through the old, in-need-of-updating kitchen to a small staircase at the back of the house. As she started up the stairs, the urge to grab her was almost uncontrollable.

"I like the view."

"What?" She spun around and was eye to eye with him, standing the step above him.

He grinned. "Sorry. I couldn't help myself." He lifted his hand to her cheek.

"Jesse…"

"One more kiss."

He moved in, and his mouth found hers. He wrapped his fingers in her hair and pressed closer to her.

There was as much urgency in her return. Her tongue found his, her hands came to his chest, and she fell against him as he moved her against the wall and stepped up to the same step with her.

She was breathless beneath him. What would stop him from taking her right in this secluded house?

Pride. Honor. Love.

He pressed his head to hers. "I'm sorry."

"Don't be."

"I can't make myself let you tell me goodbye forever," he said, gasping for breath.

"I don't want to. I've grown to have feelings for you, and I don't know what to do with that."

"Come to L.A."

She adjusted to look at him. "What? I can't leave here."

"No." He stepped back and placed his hands on her hips. "Come see me on my turf. After Thanksgiving is my last show on this tour. In L.A. Come be there."

"Jonah."

"He'll be fine with your mom." He kissed her once more. "Please."

She watched him as he stood there. How could he convince her more?

"This still isn't a good idea. We can't make it—you and me."

"Just come see me. Don't say goodbye yet if it's not what either of us want."

She let out a long breath, turned from him, and walked up the stairs.

He gathered his thoughts and followed.

She pushed open the first bedroom door and stepped in.

"My grandfather made all this."

Jesse walked over to the bed and ran his hand down the poster of the bed. "This is amazing workmanship."

"His heart was in it."

"What happens to all of this?"

"It'll have to go with the house."

A tear fell from her eye, and he moved quickly to wipe it away.

"It's all going to be okay."

"You can't say that. You don't live in my life."

He felt that more, standing in this house, than ever before.

He wished he had more words that would soothe her, but he didn't. They had one shot at this relationship, and their differences were going to tear them apart.

Just as he took a breath to speak, his cell phone rang. He pulled it from his pocket.

"Hey, Bryce."

Melissa turned to give him privacy, but the phone call seemed one-sided. Whoever was talking was talking fast and loud.

She walked to the door to leave just as he turned off his phone.

"Sorry about that," he said.

"You're a busy man."

"Yeah, and my manager just caught wind that I'd come here."

He moved to her and gathered her in his arms.

"I have to get back. The storm is growing he says, and if I don't get my flight out as soon as I can, I'll breach the contract for my show in Saint Louis."

She nodded her head. "I'll get you back."

As she turned, he reached for her arm and spun her back to him.

"I love you."

Melissa sucked in any words that she could retort.

"Don't say anything. Words come over me when I feel them," he apologized. "You need to know how deep this goes in my heart."

"Don't sing some song to me. Those are serious words."

"I don't take them lightly."

She didn't know what do with that. She broke from his grip and hurried down the stairs. He followed, but she was in a hurry to get away from him now—to get him out of her life was more like it.

Melissa was in the car before he even reached her. She put the key in the ignition and cranked, but nothing happened.

"No!"

She did it again and again. The car was dead, but her emotions had kicked into overdrive.

Jesse was standing just beyond her car door, in the snow, in a pair of very expensive and now wet shoes and a stolen coat.

Why did he have to say that? Why did he go over that line?

She opened the door and climbed out.

"I have to call to have William come jump the car."

He let out a breath on the frozen air. "Okay. They'll have to deal with that."

"Deal with it? We have no choice." She slammed the car door. "I'd flap my arms if it would get you back to your life faster."

"Is that because you don't want me?"

"It's because you're wrong to want me."

The tears that stung her eyes were frozen there as he moved in to reach for her. She couldn't have it. She couldn't have him now that he said he loved her, and he had no basis for it.

She hurried past him to get in the house.

Up the front steps she flew with him right behind her, and as she reached for the door, the board beneath her gave way and her leg went through the porch.

She let out a scream, and Jesse was right there.

"Are you okay?"

"No, you idiot, I'm not." She screamed again as she tried to pull her leg from the hole.

"Let me help you." He crouched down next to her and gently eased her foot through the board. "You tore it up pretty bad."

She looked down. Her pant leg was ripped, and her sock was bloody. "This isn't happening."

"Yes it is, and we're going to deal with it, even if you think I'm an idiot." He wrapped his arm around her. "Can you stand?"

She put her arm around his shoulder and let him pull her to her feet, but the moment she put weight on her foot, she fell against him.

"I did something to it. It might be broken."

Without another word, Jesse scooped her up into his arms and carried her into the house.

The couch was covered, but she pointed to it and he gently set her down. He knelt on the floor next to her and examined her leg.

"I'm going to take off your shoe. Your ankle is swelling."

She nodded and winced as he moved her even slightly. The moment he brushed against her ankle, her stomach rolled.

"Oh, sweetheart, you might have broken it."

She inched up to look at the already swollen ankle that was turning shades of purple.

She leaned back on the couch, kicking up dust as she did so. She reached into her coat pocket and pulled out her phone.

Jesse stood. "Do you have some bags? I could put some snow in them and put them on your ankle."

Melissa took a deep breath through the pain. "Trunk of my car. I have a survival kit. There are some bottles of water, bags, and some blankets." She fished the keys from her pocket and handed them to him.

He nodded and headed outside as she dialed William's number.

By the time Jesse walked back through the door, his hair and coat were covered in snow.

"It's really coming down now," he said as he shut the front door with his hip.

"We shouldn't have come up here."

"Oh, I don't know." He set the box he'd carried in on the coffee table. "I can't think of anything better than a Colorado mountain snowstorm and the most beautiful woman in the world, alone with me, in an amazing house."

She smiled, but the throbbing in her ankle made her wince.

"I'll get you something cold for that."

Jesse found a Ziploc bag that had some dry socks in it. He looked up at her and smiled. Melissa shrugged. She'd lived in these conditions her whole life. You prepared.

He dumped out the socks and headed for the front door. "By the way," he said as he turned the knob, "I thought you were adorable before, but after seeing this preparedness kit, you've totally won my heart. No one in L.A. is ever prepared for anything except to freshen their lipstick."

He stepped outside and shut the door behind him.

L.A. She gave it some thought. Everything there would be different. Warm weather. Beaches. Movie stars. Then she laughed. Jesse Charles was one of them—she'd nearly forgotten.

He'd become more than the poster on her son's wall. He'd become the man who filled her dreams. Not a moment in the past few weeks had gone by when she hadn't had her mind wander to him.

She found herself glancing at the folders the girls carried and the posters they had in their lockers. It made her feel closer to him. She listened to Jonah's CD in the car. And to think, after he'd played that annoying *Admirer* song so many times, she'd nearly taken her keys to the back of it so she wouldn't have to hear it.

She'd gotten upset when he said he loved her. She still didn't agree with the fact that he'd said it at all, but she felt it. She consumed him, just as he consumed her.

The cold rushed through the house when Jesse walked back through.

"Okay. Hopefully this will help." He set the bag of snow gently on her ankle.

She jumped and then eased back down on the dusty couch. "Thank you."

"Did you hurt anything else?" He said as he sat on the side of the couch..

"Just my pride."

"I assume William is on his way up?"

Melissa wrinkled up her nose. "Yes. He's plenty pissed, too."

"Because he has to drive in this?"

"No. Because I'm here with you."

Jesse nodded a slow nod of understanding. "You and William…"

"Are only friends."

"But he thinks there is more."

"He wants to think there's more. He's always taken care of me, but I'm not in love with him."

Jesse ran his fingers up her arm. "Are you sure?"

"I'm very sure."

He leaned in closer. "I'd like to be the man that takes care of you." He pulled back slightly. "Both you and Jonah."

Melissa swallowed hard because she knew what she was feeling, and it went against everything she'd ever believed in. "I'd like that."

That must have been all he needed to hear. A heartbeat later, his mouth covered hers and his fingers went into her hair. She wasn't about to pull away or make him stop. She finally admitted to herself that this was what she wanted. She wanted Jesse, and all other things would have to make sense later.

Melissa slid her hands up under his shirt. His chest was warm under her palms, and it made him gasp when she touched him.

He maneuvered his body so that he was above her, but he left one foot on the ground as to not go near her ankle.

Jesse's lips moved away from hers and he kissed her neck, trailing small kisses over her collarbone.

The moans that escaped had been buried for so long. Every touch sent electricity through her and feelings she never thought she'd feel again.

He quickly went to work unbuttoning her shirt as she tugged his free to pull it over his head.

Beneath the thin cotton was a body of chiseled muscle. His skin was smooth under her fingers, and suddenly she was aware that she had on an old cotton bra and there was no definition in her abs.

But Jesse had not once hesitated as he lay open her shirt. Wasn't that a sign of love? When they didn't see the imperfections? Or was this all lust and when it was over—it was over?

Jesse's kisses trailed between her breasts. She ran her fingers through his hair as her body became numb to the cold that blew through the house. Every touch, every kiss, every moan from Jesse made her warm.

"Come to L.A.," he said on a ragged breath as his lips pressed against the nook of her neck.

"I have obligations," she murmured, though her head clouded as to what they were.

"One weekend."

"Jonah."

"Will be fine with your mother." He pressed his mouth to hers and went about exploring with his tongue against hers.

She slid her hands down his back and over his tight buttocks. How could she have accepted that she was going to tell this man goodbye forever, when he molded to her so perfectly?

"I'll be there."

Jesse pulled back just far enough to gaze down at her. "Promise?"

"Wouldn't miss it."

As he moved back against her, they heard the sound of tires on the snow.

Jesse quickly moved off of her and searched for his T-shirt as she frantically began to button her shirt. Only a moment later, William burst through the front door.

"Are you okay?" he asked, walking right past Jesse to Melissa.

"I'm fine. I fell though that board."

"I knew I should have come right back up here and fixed it." He lifted the melted bag of snow from her ankle, which now looked worse than it had. "We need to get you to a doctor."

"I need to get Jesse to the airport."

William turned and looked at him, his eyes narrow. "You're leaving in this weather?"

"I have a concert tomorrow. I'm under contract to be there."

William gritted his teeth. "Just great." He looked back at Melissa. "I'm going to go jump the car. Don't you move."

She nodded, but she didn't like his tone. Not to her and certainly not to Jesse. None of this was Jesse's fault.

William headed toward the door and then turned to Jesse. "C'mon. I'll need some help."

Jesse didn't have a lot of experience with principals. He'd been tutored most his life. But this one scared the hell out of him.

William didn't like him, but he was used to having critics. But it seemed important for him to win this one over.

He'd meant it when he told Melissa he loved her. Perhaps it had been too premature to say, but he couldn't help himself.

William went to his car and popped open the trunk. He pulled out a pair of jumper cables. "Pop the hood on her car."

Jesse nodded and walked around Melissa's car as William opened his car door and pulled the lever for his hood.

He handed Jesse the ends of the cables. "Here, hook these up."

Jesse took the ends and stood there. He saw William's cheeks turn redder under the layer of cold.

"You expect to take care of her and Jonah, and you can't jump a car?"

"I've just never had to deal with this."

William huffed over toward him and took the cables. He attached them and then walked to his car and did the same.

"I'm going to start my car. When I say, you get in and start hers."

Jesse nodded. Maybe he wasn't cut out for this taking-care-of-people thing. After all, he had a staff that took care of just him.

When William gave him a signal, he turned the key, but nothing happened. He nodded for him to do it again, but again—nothing.

William got out of his car and walked around to where Jesse sat behind the wheel. Jesse moved out, and William tried his hand at starting the car.

Jesse felt slightly better knowing it didn't start for him either.

"Damn. I told her she needed a new car. This one is plum wore out and she refuses." He climbed out of the car and hurried to his to turn it off. "I'll have to have it towed."

"I have my truck at her place. I bought it to keep in town. She should use it until she can get this fixed."

"You bought a truck to keep here?"

"Yes."

"Why? Do you really think you can move in on her like this? What kind of game are you playing?"

Why did he feel as if he were on trial? He was a grown man, but he felt belittled by this man standing before him in a dress coat.

Jesse could buy the town if he wanted. How was it one man could make him feel so small?

Then it hit him. Because this man loved the same woman he did, only he could give her the life she was used to. Jesse was just messing it up.

"I don't want to cause her any pain. I care for her."

"You've been around her three times."

"Relationships have to start somewhere."

William walked at him. Jesse planted his feet in the snow just in case he came to take a swing.

"She's not some Hollywood floosy."

"I know. I respect who she is. That's what I love about her."

He inched closer. "Love?"

Jesse swallowed hard. "Listen. If she tells me to go, I go. But for now, I want to be part of her life."

William sucked in a breath, and it came back out as a cloud on the cold air. "Let's get you to your flight," he grunted and walked back into the house.

By the time they'd made it into the house, Melissa had fallen asleep on the couch. It was no wonder. He was used to long days that never ended—she wasn't that person. She probably had a set bedtime every night, just like her son.

William walked to her side as Jesse shut the door. He knelt down next to her. "Honey, the car is dead."

She stirred and opened her eyes. She focused in on him. "Dead? As in the battery?"

"I don't think it's the battery this time."

"Damn."

"I told you that you needed to replace it. It's old and not made for these conditions."

She nodded and wiped her eyes. "Where's Jesse?"

"I'm here," he quickly spoke up.

"I hope you're not going to be late."

William shook his head. "We'll get him to the airport. You're keeping his truck until we buy you a new one."

His voice was stern and definite.

"Let me get you off this couch," he said.

Melissa looked at him and then up at Jesse. "Can you carry me out?"

Jesse's heart went out to her. What an awkward position she was in, having them both there fussing over her. "Yeah."

He moved in toward the couch, and William backed away.

"Put your arm over my neck."

He lifted her from the couch and, with ease, carried her out to William's car.

William hurried around and opened the back door so Jesse could set her down and she could rest her foot up on the seat.

As he set her down, she looked up at him and smiled. "Thank you," she said softly.

"Get comfy."

The urge to kiss her at that moment was nearly irresistible, but with William literally breathing down his neck, he thought better of it and stepped back.

William stepped up. "I'm going to lock up the house. Do you still have a blanket in your car?"

She nodded.

He looked up at Jesse. "Find the blanket. It's yellow. We'll prop it up so she can sit with her foot up."

William headed back to the house, and Jesse went to find the yellow blanket. He was sure "blanket" would have sufficed in the description, but William letting him know that he knew she had a blanket and exactly what color it was had been his way of keeping control over the situation. There was an underlying tone of *I'm her man and you're in the way.*

Jesse found the blanket and walked back to William's car.

Melissa had fallen asleep again. He felt terrible having kept her up all night. She was well past the twenty-four hour mark by now.

As he gazed down at her, William hurried down the front steps. "Don't just stand there if you're in a hurry."

He took the blanket from Jesse and stirred Melissa awake. He tucked the blanket between her and the door so she could recline. Then he got into the car, and Jesse followed suit.

Moments later, Melissa was asleep again, and Jesse watched her as William began their decent down the mountain and out of Aspen Creek toward Grand Junction.

"Does she have the keys to your truck?" William asked, his eyes focused on the road.

"No." Jesse dug into his pocket and pulled out the keys. He held them in his hand. "She can keep it as long as she needs to. I know things are tough right now for her…"

"Damn straight they are."

Jesse only nodded. This man didn't like him, and he made that clear.

"Thank you for taking me to the airport."

"If it's what she needs me to do, then I do it."

The point was taken. None of this was a favor to Jesse.

The drive was cold and quiet. He hadn't realized just how much a snowstorm would hinder the drive, but it had. It was evening by the time William got him to the airport.

Jesse zipped up his *borrowed* coat and looked back at Melissa.

"I won't wake her, but let her know I'll call her later."

William only nodded.

Jesse handed him the keys to his truck. "Thank you for everything. I'm sorry if we ruined any of your plans for today."

Jesse opened the door and stepped out.

"Hey," William called, and Jesse ducked his head back into the car. "I'm sorry I've been suck a jerk." He looked back at Melissa. "She's very important to me, and I don't want to see her get hurt."

Jesse nodded. "She's important to me too, and I feel the same way." He shut the door to the car and headed back to his life—his miserable pop-star life.

Chapter Ten

Melissa heard William's voice in her ear, and she stirred.

Her neck was stiff from having slept so long in the back seat of the car.

"Where are we?"

"Hospital," William said as he reached a hand in to help her out.

She looked around and realized it was only the two of them. "Jesse?"

"I dropped him off at the airport."

She sat straight up and coursing pain shot through her ankle. "Why didn't he say goodbye?"

"I didn't see any reason to wake you."

"You?" She pulled herself up further, gritting her teeth against the pain. "How was that your decision to make?"

"I just wanted to get you here with the least amount of pain."

"I'm fine," she said as she winced.

His lips pursed. "Maybe you should fix the buttons on your shirt before we get inside."

She looked down and noticed she'd buttoned her shirt wrong after she and Jesse had hurried to dress quickly.

She huffed out a breath and adjusted the buttons.

William shook his head. "Melissa, what were you doing up there?"

"It is none of your business. I'm an adult. I will be with whomever I want."

"But…"

"Don't you lecture me. I'm not one of your students, and I am not your wife."

William only shook his head. "Let's get inside and get this looked at."

William helped her to the edge of the seat and then went and retrieved a wheelchair. He hoisted her out of the car and into the chair and pushed her into the emergency room.

Two hours later, as the long day inched into night, Melissa was released with a pair of crutches and a severely sprained ankle.

William filled her prescription and then helped her back into the car. She'd done her best to not even speak to him. She was furious.

They pulled into her driveway, and William hurried around the car.

Patsy opened the front door. "Is she okay?"

"Sprained ankle," he answered as he opened the car door. "Let me help you."

Melissa batted away his hand. "I'm fine. I can get this on my own."

She scooted to the edge of the seat and took the crutches he'd pulled out of the car for her.

"I'll walk in with you," he said softly.

"William, go home. I think you've aggravated me enough today."

She hobbled to the front step on her crutches where her mother waited for her. She hated the feeling of being dependent on sticks under her arms to make her mobile.

"Melissa, what happened?" her mother asked.

"I fell through that board on the porch."

"I thought William was going to fix that. Well, she's showing it tomorrow. We'll need to fix it."

"Patsy, I'll head up tomorrow after school and take care of it," William called from the driveway.

Her mother nodded as Melissa made it into the house.

"Melissa," he called to her as he headed up to the door. "Jesse wanted you to have these." He handed her the keys to the truck. "He wants you to drive it until we get you something else."

She took the keys and put them in her pocket.

"I'll pick you up in the morning, if you'd like."

"Go home, William. I'll be fine," she said as she passed by her mother and went into the house to sit down.

Melissa hobbled to the kitchen and pulled down a glass to fill with water to take her prescription. Her ankle throbbed, and her anger was making her sick to her stomach.

"What was all of that about?" her mother asked as she walked into the kitchen.

"What?"

"You were rude to William."

Melissa filled the glass and proceeded to fight with the lid on the medicine bottle. "William Scott has a unique way of meddling in other people's business where he doesn't belong."

She continued to struggle with the lid until her mother took the bottle from her and opened it.

"Thank you."

"Where is Jesse?"

"I have no idea. My car broke down. William had to come and get us, and he took Jesse to the airport and didn't even wake me from the back seat to say goodbye."

Melissa swallowed back the pills, and her mother closed the bottle.

"William's feelings are hurt. He's had eyes for you since high school. Of course this is going to upset him."

"Well, I'm over it. A nice, young man wants to be with me, and I have this nut job pushing him away."

Her mother leaned against the counter. "How do you feel about Jesse?"

Melissa huffed out a breath. "I really like him."

"That's all that matters. He's good people. I can see that."

"So why can't William just let me be happy?"

Her mother set the prescription bottle behind the sink. "If you choose Jesse, William will be happy for you. But, for now, he's not used to sharing you."

"Sharing me? I'm not his to share."

Her mother touched her arm. "Just be considerate of his feelings."

Melissa didn't need to hear that. William was not part of this relationship she was having, so he needed to butt out.

She adjusted and started out of the kitchen. "Jesse wants me to go to L.A. for his final concert after Thanksgiving. Would you mind keeping Jonah?"

Her mother smiled. "You're going to go stay with a man?"

"Don't make me feel like some teenager who doesn't…"

"I didn't say it was bad. I think it's time for you to move on." She smiled.

"I like him, Mom."

"I know. Go to bed. You've had a very long day."

Melissa nodded and made her way, slowly, down the hall. She sat down on her bed and lifted her foot up.

Jonah appeared at her door.

"Hey, kiddo. You should be in bed."

He rubbed his arm. "Are you okay?"

"Yes, just sprained my ankle." She adjusted the pillows, putting one under her foot.

"I heard you tell grandma that you were going to go to see Jesse."

She let out a deep breath. "Yes. He asked me to visit him."

Jonah nodded. "I like him mom. He treats you good."

That was certainly a lot for a young boy to think about. She patted the bed next to her, and Jonah crawled up next to her.

"I don't know that it will work out—long term, that is."

"Why?"

"We don't come from the same kind of life."

"People learn to adjust. We learned to live without Daddy."

Melissa pulled him close to her. "You're right. We did." She kissed the top of his head. "I like him."

"He likes you, too. He told me that he'll call you tomorrow, and Bryce will make plans for you to visit."

Melissa pulled back and looked at him. "You talked to him?"

"He called to check on you. He says I can call him anytime, too."

"Don't you go bothering him."

"Mom," he whined. "I won't." Jonah jumped down from the bed and walked to the door. "Mom, I think it's cool that he likes you. Not just because he's Jesse. Well—but, because he's Jesse."

She laughed. "I understand."

He gave her a wave and headed off, just as Melissa's phone rang.

"Hello, Jesse," she said softly.

"How are you? Did you break it? I would have said goodbye, but…"

"I know." She settled against her pillow. "William was in rare form today. I'm sorry."

"He's watching out for you."

She let out a sigh. "I'm a grownup. I can do that for myself."

"What about your ankle?"

"Sprained. I'm on crutches for a little bit, but I'm okay."

"That's good." He went silent for a moment, and Melissa even checked the signal on her phone to make sure the call was still connected. Then she heard him breathe. "I still want you to come see me. But I'd understand if…"

"Jesse, I'll be there."

"Really?"

"I miss you already." It felt good to admit that aloud, only now it left a hollow feeling in her chest. The thought of them on the couch, his hands on her skin, his mouth against hers…she had to remember to breathe.

"I'm glad to hear that. Hey, Bryce is going to call you tomorrow to set up your trip."

"Okay, I'll make sure to answer."

He laughed. "I can't wait to hold you."

Her heart rate kicked up. "I can't wait either."

"I know I promised I wouldn't say it again, but, Melissa, I love you."

She wasn't sure what to say in response. She knew that the feelings she had for him were shifting in that direction, but to say the words…

"I'll let you get some rest," he said quickly. "I'll call you tomorrow."

"Good night."

Melissa was surprised when Bryce called before she'd left for school. He was a thorough assistant.

She'd leave the week after Thanksgiving to attend the final show of Jesse's tour. Just thinking about it made her hands shake. It was very clear that she'd be staying with Jesse at his house. Everything would change then. Everything.

Before she left her bedroom, she took one last look in the mirror. Was she ready to completely be with another man?

Was this the right step?

Could she give her heart, her body, and her son to a man so much younger than her?

She put her hand to her chest. She wanted to.

Now all she had to do was go to school and tell William she needed a couple days off so she could go to L.A. and sleep with Jesse.

As she stood there, looking in the mirror, her cheeks flushed. Of course, she'd never use those words, but that would be what he heard.

She waited until the end of school to approach William, mostly because he'd avoided her all day long.

When she hobbled into his office, he wasn't there.

"He said he was going to head up to your grandfather's and fix the porch. Your mom called and said they had an offer on the property," his secretary said as Melissa stood there balanced on her crutches.

That was some of the saddest news she'd ever heard, and it had to come from the secretary.

She puffed up her cheeks and let out the ragged breath that had built in her lungs.

It looked like she was taking a drive up the mountain.

William was crouched on the front porch when she pulled up to the house. He looked over his shoulder and hurried toward the truck as she wiggled her way out of the seat.

"What are you doing up here?" he started in. "You shouldn't be out here. You should be home with your foot up."

"I needed to talk to you, and you were already gone."

"Maybe I didn't want to see you."

The thought had crossed her mind and now, standing in front of her grandfather's house with her foot freezing in the snow, she realized she should have just waited until tomorrow.

"I needed to clear some time off."

"You came up here to ask for time off?"

"The Thursday and Friday after Thanksgiving."

He rubbed the back of his neck with his hand. "That's next week."

"I know it's short notice."

The look in his eyes changed from consideration to realization. "Where are you going?"

She took a breath to calm her nerves. "L.A."

His jaw tensed, and he took a step toward her. "You're going to him? You're going to be with him?"

"Yes."

"You're leaving your son home so you can go have a weekend of sex with a man who will never love you like I do?"

She couldn't help it. Her hand came through the air and across his face. And the moment she'd smacked him, she covered her mouth.

"I'm sorry."

He rubbed his cheek. "I deserved it."

"William, what happened to us?"

"Jesse Charles."

She shook her head. "He didn't ruin this."

William dropped his hand and took another step closer to her. "I don't want to see you get hurt." He touched her cheek with his frozen fingertips. "Go. See what it's all about."

"Really?"

He nodded and stepped in until their bodies nearly touched. "I'll be here when you come back."

He leaned in and brushed his lips to hers.

The shock should have had her pushing him away, but she was so confused she didn't know what to do.

He rested his forehead to hers. "Go have your weekend and then come home to me."

"This isn't just a weekend."

He pulled back. "Come back and marry me."

This time she did shove him back. "You're telling me you think so little of this that I'll go have sex with a man and then come home and marry you?"

"He's not the right man for you."

"And you are?"

"I've been the one here. I'm the one who has taken care of you and Jonah. I have your best interest at heart."

"So does Jesse."

"He's young."

"He's mature."

"He's going to hurt you. When he does, I'll still be here." He turned and walked back to the house.

Melissa fell back into the seat of the truck and quickly drove away.

The man was delusional. Did he really expect that if she was going to go spend the weekend with a man that she'd hurry home and marry him?

Was this what everyone would think?

Was she now just some whore?

Tears began to well in her eyes.

Well, to hell with everyone then. She was going to Jesse. And if he broke her heart then she'd live with that, but not because William Scott said he would.

And she'd be damned if she'd consider marrying William now.

Chapter Eleven

Thanksgiving came and went. Melissa and Jonah had sat and watched the parade, which was tradition, and her mother had put out a lovely spread. The only thing missing this year was William and his mother.

She hadn't had it in her heart to invite him, and he hadn't asked.

He'd stayed away from church and again, unless he had to talk to her, he didn't even come near her at school.

Monday morning she limped around her classroom. All she wore now was an ankle brace, but she was hoping that by Thursday, when she flew to L.A., she wouldn't need it.

Melissa was situating the room for the lesson she'd present six times that day when there was a knock on the door.

She turned to see Emmy standing there in all of her bohemian glory.

"How's your ankle?" she asked.

"Much better."

"I hear you're leaving to fly out to L.A. this weekend."

Melissa plastered a smile on her lips and nodded. "Yes."

"I think you'll have a great time." She moved into the room. "I was thinking, if you're up for it, I'd love to give you a makeover. I'm working over at Heidi's Salon after school."

Melissa laughed. "I didn't know you did that, too."

Emmy sat down on the top of a desk and adjusted the many bangle bracelets on her arm. "Artist in many forms. Anyway, I figured, not that you don't look beautiful, but maybe I could give you a California look. You know—not a Colorado winter look."

She hadn't thought about it. She was sure she was in for culture shock.

Emmy stood. "Besides, I suppose you'll be photographed a lot. We might as well show them just how beautiful you are. Again, not that you're not."

That had brought up a point Melissa hadn't thought about. She'd be with one of the biggest names in the music industry. Did she think this would be an intimate time with Jesse? Yes, she had.

Emmy stood and quickly walked to her. "Are you okay?"

"Yes. I just hadn't considered the part where I'd be seen."

Emmy laughed and her eyes softened. "You see him differently than the rest of the world sees him. You're in love with him."

She was desperately in need of sitting down.

"This is all so crazy. Maybe I shouldn't go."

"Like hell!" Emmy quickly covered her mouth. "I'm sorry. I mean, yes you should."

"I don't feel so well."

Emmy patted her on the back. "You'll be fine." She stood back up. "Now, can I ask you for a favor?"

"Sure."

She moved in closer. "If you're serious about Jesse, will you help me get William to notice me?"

That brought a genuine smile to Melissa's face. "Really?"

"Yes, really. Until he knows you're okay, he'll never look my way. But...I really like him."

Melissa thought perhaps it was that his ears were burning because he walked through the door at that moment.

"Can I talk to you?" he asked, narrowing his eyes at Melissa.

"Sure."

Emmy lifted then dropped her shoulders. "I'll let you be. Can you come by today about five?"

Melissa nodded.

"I'll see you then." She walked by William. "Have a good day, Mr. Scott."

But it was as if he never heard her. He walked right up to Melissa and threw down a newspaper.

"You're not going!"

"How dare you…"

He shoved the paper toward her. JESSE CHARLES AND SUPERMODEL GIRLFRIEND TO MARRY

No words came to her. Nothing.

"He's playing you, and you're falling into it. I'm not going to let you go through with this."

"I'm sure that's not true."

"Are you really going to ignore this? You think you can just fly out there, sleep with him, and he'll forget all about this."

Melissa picked up the paper and tossed it at him. "I think…" she paused to suck back the tears that threatened, "I think I'll talk to him first."

Melissa had texted him six times throughout the day. Her message wasn't returned until nearly four o'clock. *Call Bryce.*

She sat in his truck outside of her house, looking down at the phone. Could the message be more cold?

William must have been right. Why would he…

Her phone rang, and the caller ID showed Bryce's name.

"Hello." Her voice quivered.

"Oh, hell, you're crying."

"I'm not crying."

"Uh-huh. Girl, I know tears."

She laughed through the tears he'd heard. She assumed he was gay when she'd met him, but as soon as he said that, she was most assured of it.

"Listen, he's with the lawyers right now so he can't talk to you."

"Lawyers?"

"You saw the news?"

Melissa batted the tears from her eyelashes. "I saw it."

"Well, it's not true. He met that model one time, backstage. He's not seeing her. He's never been with her. He certainly isn't marrying her."

"How do I know…"

"You trust your heart. He'll call you when he's out of the office and done with rehearsal. But he wanted me to assure you that none of it's true. Understand?"

"I understand."

"Okay, sweetheart. By the way, you and I have a few hours on Friday to do some shopping while he goes to the arena for last minute rehearsals. Ever been to Rodeo Dr.?"

"Never," she said on a laugh. "I've only seen it from the *Pretty Woman* movie."

"It all rings true. They aren't nice to people, but I have a slush fund to spend on you. You're going to look fabulous."

As soon as they hung up, she was able to breathe easier.

It wasn't true. He wasn't marrying some supermodel. Jesse Charles was still in love with her.

She hurried into the house to change her clothes. Emmy was expecting her and was going to make her look fabulous. L.A. wasn't going to know what hit them when she showed up on his arm. Better yet, she was going to wow the clothes off of Jesse.

Melissa walked, very slowly, into the school the next morning a new woman. Emmy had done miracles to her hair. There were subtle highlights and layers. It had been years since she'd taken a blow dryer to her hair and created style, but it was an amazing difference. Emmy had arched her eyebrows and even polished her nails into a beautiful French manicure. All she'd charged her was the promise to talk to William—and a cup of coffee at Molly's.

It had been nearly ten o'clock by the time she'd gotten home. Her mother and son had approved of her new look. Now all she had to do was convince William to leave her alone and entertain the idea of getting involved with Emmy.

As she walked down the hall to her classroom, William came around the corner.

He'd taken a double take before he stopped. "I almost didn't recognize you."

"Oh really?"

He pursed his lips, looked at the ground, and then back up to her. "You look beautiful."

"Emmy works wonders."

"Emmy did this?"

She reached up and touched the side of his head. "Looks like you should go visit her, too. Getting a little shaggy." She started past him. "She works at Heidi's."

She opened the door to her classroom, and he followed her in."

"I wanted to apologize. I shouldn't have…"

"William, you're looking out for me. I understand that."

"Then one more time I'll ask you not to go."

She looked up at him and shook her head. "You came in here to tell me that again after you apologized?"

"No." He looked down at his hands. "Actually, I thought I'd offer you a ride to Grand Junction on Thursday morning."

"You want to drive me to the airport where I'll be getting on a plane to go see a man?"

He pursed his lips. "Yes."

"That's very thoughtful. Thank you."

Wednesday night, Melissa stood in front of her closet and stared at her clothes. This was the wardrobe of a biology teacher, not the full closet of the girlfriend of one of the sexiest men in the world. If Emmy was right about people taking pictures of her, and no doubt publicizing them, she was toast.

She sat down on her bed and shook her head. She wasn't sure who was going to be more embarrassed, Jesse or her.

At that moment, her phone rang and it was Jesse. She lay back on the bed and answered it.

"Hello."

"Hey, sweetheart. Rumor had it you were getting ready to leave town." His voice was soft, and the background was quiet. That was new.

"Actually, I was having second thoughts. I don't own any California clothes."

He chuckled. "I don't care. You can come in that frog vest, if you want. I just can't wait to hold you in my arms. I miss you."

How was it that this amazingly sexy musician was so smitten with her? "I'm nervous."

"Don't be. I'm a gentleman. I'll never make you do anything you don't want to do."

Melissa lifted her hand and looked over her nails, but it was her wedding ring that caught her attention. "No, it's not that. Emmy has it in my head that there will be press and…"

"There will be. Is that a problem?"

She sat up on the bed. "I didn't think it was going to be. But, Jesse, I'm not someone worthy of that kind of attention on your arm."

"You're the woman I want to be with."

"Why?"

"I really don't want to go through that again. I just want you here in my arms. I want to hold you and kiss you. I want to tell you a million times that I love you, even if you don't reciprocate the feelings. And trust me, if you don't come out here, I'll show up at school and sweep you off your feet. No matter what, I want to be with you."

She sighed. "I'm sorry. I have a little insecurity over this."

"My mother wants to meet you when you're here."

That sent her heart into her throat. "Oh, I hadn't thought about having to meet your family."

"She can't be anymore opinionated than William was."

Melissa closed her eyes tight. "I hope he wasn't rude to you."

"He cares for you. It actually gives me some peace of mind to know he cares as much as he does."

That was very sincere. This man was a catch.

"I'll let you get back to packing," he said.

"How did you know that was what I was doing?"

"Jonah."

Melissa stood. "I told him not to bother you."

"Don't be upset. He is a complete gentleman when he calls. He always makes sure I'm not busy. Besides, I really enjoy talking to him. Trust me, I know that I'm not just building a relationship with you. I have to earn his heart, too."

Earn his heart. This man was good with the words.

"I'll see you tomorrow. And, Melissa, I love you."

The line was silent before she could even say goodbye. She looked back into her closest and pulled out the frog vest. No, she'd never wear it in public, but she sure as heck was going to pack it just to be funny.

Chapter Twelve

Melissa woke early, got ready, and packed up her last minute essentials. As she stood in front of the mirror, giving herself one more look, she realized that no matter what happened this weekend she'd come home a changed woman.

She heard the doorbell and her mother's voice as she answered. Melissa sucked in a breath and let it out slowly as she adjusted the collar on her shirt.

Again only one thing stood out. Her wedding ring still adorned her finger.

She looked down at it and gave the thin band of gold a twist. Then she grasped it between her fingers and pulled it off.

Melissa swallowed hard. It hadn't been off her finger since the day Martin had put it there.

As she held it in her hand, she bit down on her lip to keep it from quivering. It was the right thing to do. Martin had been gone for three years. Time was moving on without her, and for Jonah's sake as well as her own, she needed to start moving with it.

She set it down on the dresser in front of the picture she kept of the two of them.

"I'll never stop loving you. But it's time for me to move on."

Melissa took another breath, and it felt as though her lungs were clear. She pushed back her shoulders, and they didn't seem so heavy.

It was as if he were telling her to go.

The drive to Grand Junction was quiet. William had bought Melissa a coffee at Molly's on the way out of town, and she'd focused on it and not on the butterflies jumping around in her stomach.

In a few hours she'd be transported to a whole new world, and suddenly she wasn't sure she was ready for that.

But she was ready to spend the weekend with Jesse—in every capacity. She'd told Martin it was time for her to move on. Now she just had to convince herself.

William pulled up in front of the small airport and parked his truck at the curb.

"I have a meeting or I'd walk you in," he offered as he climbed out of the truck.

"I'll be fine." Melissa slowly slid from the seat and gently landed pressure on her ankle. It was feeling much better, but it still ached.

William pulled her luggage from the back and set it on the curb. "Guess I should have asked before. Do you have everything? Your ticket? Some money? A…"

"I have everything. Thank you."

William nodded and rubbed the back of his head with his hand.

"You call me if you need anything. Anything at all."

"I will." Melissa moved in and wrapped her arms around him. After all, he was her dearest friend. "Thank you."

As she pulled back, William's hands came to her face. He pulled her face to his and pressed his lips to hers.

The shock inhibited her movement.

When he pulled back, he let out a long breath. "Go. Have fun. Let go of all the pain of the past few years." He walked back around the truck, and she turned to watch him. "Come home and marry me."

He didn't wait for a reaction. He climbed back into the truck and drove away.

Melissa stood there. Her lips still tingled from the kiss. Her heart pounded out of adrenaline and anger.

She picked up her suitcase and walked into the airport. It was time to move on. That much was for sure. And to hell with William Scott.

Melissa purchased a snack on the airplane, but she found it hard to even think of food. The closer she got to California, the more nervous she became.

When the flight landed at LAX, Melissa was transported into an entirely different world.

It wasn't as if she'd never traveled before, but the truth was, she'd never traveled often. In the past three years she hadn't been anywhere but Utah for scouting events.

The air was already much warmer, but she looked around and noticed people were still wearing sweaters. The thought made her laugh. Jonah would have been in shorts, yet the November weather had Californians bundling up.

Before she headed to the baggage claim, she stopped in the bathroom to fix herself up.

At first glance, she thought she looked tired. But then she was always critical of herself. The long layers Emmy had cut into her hair still flipped just right. She ran her fingers through her strands to give some body to them.

Melissa opened her purse and found her pearl lip balm. She applied it, ran her fingers under her eyes to freshen her eyeliner, and gave her blouse an adjustment.

This was as good as it was going to get. No matter where you took her, Melissa would always be a small town teacher—inside and out.

Melissa walked toward the carousel where her luggage was to land. Other passengers from her flight had gathered around.

She looked for a sign with her name on it. Jesse had said someone would pick her up. She'd expected Bryce, but he wasn't there either.

When her bag descended the ramp, she reached for it at the same time a man in a baseball cap reached for it.

"I got this," he said.

"Thank you." She turned to reach for it and noticed the smile of the man who had helped her.

He had on a button-up shirt, which was untucked, and a pair of Levi jeans. His baseball cap had seen better days, and his beautiful grey eyes were shielded with sunglasses.

"I thought you were sending someone for me," she said softly.

He leaned in closer to her and brushed her lips with a kiss. "I only have a few days with you. I'm not going to miss a moment."

He slid his arm around her waist and pulled her suitcase beside him.

Melissa looked around. No one noticed the man who kept her close to his side. "Are you alone?"

"Behind us about ten feet."

She looked over her shoulder, and the big brawly man who followed them gave her a nod.

She smiled briefly. "I guess this is a big gamble for you, isn't it? Bringing an average woman into your life?" She hadn't meant for it to sound snide, but it certainly had come across that way.

"No gamble. The gamble in my life was asking you to come and you telling me no."

"I still think that might have been the right answer."

He nodded as he continued to walk toward the parking garage. "I hope to make you change your mind."

When they reached the parking garage, Jesse pulled his keys from his pocket and pushed a button. The lights on the black BMW down the aisle lit up. He pushed another button and the trunk lifted.

The truck he'd purchased to keep in Colorado was modest. Looking at the beautiful car before her, Melissa quickly realized he was in his element. Flashy and fast—she was slow and plain.

Jesse hoisted her luggage into the trunk and pushed down the door, and then he pulled her into his arms. His mouth came to hers quickly, and she sucked in a breath.

As soon as she relaxed into the kiss, he deepened it. His tongue sought out hers, and her head spun with the delight of him.

He pulled back, only far enough to rest his forehead to hers. "I'm so glad you came. I've missed you something terrible."

Melissa swallowed hard. "I'm nervous."

"Don't be."

"People think you're getting married and…"

Jesse let out a long, ragged breath. "You can't believe that. You can't let them get into your head."

She nodded. "I know. This is all new to me."

He smiled. "I know it's not what you're used to, and I know this whole thing is just a little crazy, but my heart tells me differently. It's telling me this *is* the real thing. That you're the real thing." He brushed her hair away from her face and rested his palm against her cheek. "Don't let the media and the gossip push you away. I'd give this all up for you."

That made her chuckle. "I doubt that."

Jesse dropped his hands, and she could see the crease in his eyebrows through his sunglasses. "Let me prove my love and loyalty to you. I promised not to break Jonah's heart. I have no intentions of breaking yours."

He gave her another quick kiss and then opened her door, waited for her to climb into the car, and then walked around to the other side and climbed in.

Jesse backed out of the parking space, hit a button on the dash, and the top opened up and tucked itself neatly in the back.

Melissa pulled her sunglasses out of her purse and flashed him the biggest smile she could. She was ready for her adventure.

Jesse gave a wave to the man who had followed them out of the airport and was now behind them in a similar car. They left the airport and headed southwest on the 405.

When Jesse maneuvered onto the highway, which was already packed with cars, Melissa laughed aloud.

"What's so funny?"

She shook her head. "The 405! The signs!" She laughed again. "This is like some fantasy. Hollywood. Beverly Hills. Santa Monica. All of this is real, and you live in the middle of it."

He nodded slowly. "I never thought about it being all that. I'm taken with the scenery from your grandfather's house."

Melissa sat back in her seat, the smile still permeating her face. "Oh, that's the best. I'd never give up home. But this…" She spread her arms out wide. "This is awesome."

This time, Jesse laughed as traffic slowed to crawl. He reached his hand over to her hair. "I like this, by the way."

"My hair?"

"Don't get me wrong. Those curls were part of why I fell in love with you, but this flippy thing," he said as he let a piece of her hair slide through his fingers. "It's sexy."

Heat began to build in her stomach, and her heart rate kicked up. This was the beginning. In a few hours, or even less, she'd be wrapped in this man's arms, and it would be her call if it went further.

There suddenly was no doubt in her mind; she wanted it to go much, much further.

Melissa had never seen traffic crawl before. It took them nearly an hour on the highway to get from the airport to the exit Jesse finally took. The entire time his guard was only a car behind them.

Jesse drove through a neighborhood where the houses were obscured by high walls and gates, but Melissa could see the peaks of the roofs and knew the massive sizes of the houses. She couldn't help but wonder who lived in each house.

Jesse slowed the car in front of a house with a gate and a wall. He pushed a button near his review mirror, and the gate swung open.

There before her, Melissa saw a house like no other. It was the size of at least four of her houses and was so much prettier.

Jesse drove around to the side, pushed another button, and the garage door went up. He pulled in, parked the BMW next to an enormous black Hummer, and shut the door.

He turned to Melissa. "Home sweet home."

"I'm embarrassed that you've been to mine."

"Why?"

She shook her head and looked around at the garage. Her garage had snow shovels and a lawn mower. There were skate boards and bicycles. This one looked clean and well kept. It didn't look like a garage at all.

"Your house is amazing."

He laughed as he climbed out of the car. "C'mon. This is only the garage. Let me show you around."

He walked around the car and opened her door. He held out his hand and took hers.

She slid from the seat and again right into his arms. "Thank you for coming," he said as he dipped his head for a kiss.

Jesse took her by the hand and led her up the stairs and through a door that went right into the kitchen.

Melissa knew she'd gasped aloud when Jesse turned to look at her.

"Wow." It might have sounded dumb, but it summed up her feelings. "I've never seen a kitchen like this."

Jesse laughed. "I don't use it myself. I can't even make a PB and J."

Melissa exchanged glances with him. "I don't believe that."

"Okay. That's all I can make. Consuela comes in once a week and makes all my meals, and Bryce's, and we eat those." He walked over to the subzero refrigerator and pulled open the doors. It was stocked with water, Red Bull, and containers of meals, just like he'd said.

What she wouldn't give for that luxury, she thought.

Melissa's head turned when she heard footsteps on the tile floor. She smiled when she saw Bryce walk into the room.

"Oh, she's here!" He hurried over to her and wrapped her in a big hug. "I was afraid you'd chicken out."

"Almost."

Bryce stepped back and looked her over. "Honey, I love the hair." He ran his fingers through it. "It's beautiful."

"Thank you."

Jesse pulled out two bottles of water from the refrigerator and handed one to Melissa. "You know, if any other man fondled my girlfriend like that, I'd kick his ass."

"Yeah, I'm safe," Bryce laughed. He walked toward the island and set down an enormous, leather-bound book. "Tyson called four times." He flipped open the book, took out a sheet of paper, and handed it to Jesse.

Jesse scanned it over and then wadded the paper up and threw it in the trash. "I told him I have a guest. We can do business next week. I want to spend time with Melissa."

"Didn't I tell him that?" Bryce held up both his hands as if to stop Jesse from talking further. "That man is an ass. You'd be better going independent." He closed the book and tucked it back up under his arm. "Either way, you're expected at the arena tomorrow for a sound check, and me and your girlfriend have a date on Rodeo, remember?" He shifted his eyes to her.

"I remember."

With a wave of his hand, he walked out another door which Melissa could see led to a patio where there was a swimming pool.

She looked back at Jesse. "If you have things you need to do…"

He gathered her in his arms. "All I need to do is this."

His lips met hers. This kiss was slow and soft, as if there were no reason to hurry—no eyes watching.

Melissa moved in closer to him and lifted her arms around his neck. Jesse slowly moved his hands down her back and over her bottom. She jerked at the movement, but settled against him.

She needed to free her mind of everything. This weekend, she wasn't a teacher. Jonah was safe and taken care of with her mother. She could relax. This weekend, she was Jesse's girlfriend—Martin's wife was something of the past. She'd said goodbye to that when she'd left the house.

Her body began to mold against his as he pulled her even closer. One hand held her close low on her back. The other hand moved to her hair.

His tongue moved against hers, and the need for him grew deeper.

Jesse finally broke the kiss and rested his head against hers. "God, if I don't stop, we'll never get out of this house." He pressed another gentle kiss to her lips. "I love you. I want you to know this weekend wasn't about getting you out here to have sex with you."

Her mind was still spinning, but she only nodded her head.

"I promised my mother I'd bring you out to meet her."

Melissa sighed. "Nothing takes away sexual heat like the mention of someone's mother."

Jesse laughed. "I know." He pulled her into him and embraced her. "This is so right. Do you feel that? You're meant to be in my arms."

She didn't want to speak. The wrong words would come out. Instead she just held on as long as she could. She was happy, and she knew she was in love. It needed to be all that mattered at that moment because already she knew she didn't fit in this city, this house, or in his life.

Jesse had fetched her bag from the car and carried it inside.

"I'll show you upstairs." He led her through the house, which was pristine with white walls, marble floors, and plush carpet in the living room off the entrance. Thank goodness Jonah wasn't with her, she was afraid she'd make a mess of the house as it was.

Jesse pushed the door open to a room and set the bag down. "I had Bryce prepare this room for you."

It was lovely. She could see some redecorating in her own bedroom after having this. The duvet was so pristine on the bed she was sure it was new and on the night stand there was a vase of roses and a card.

Enjoy your visit, Love Bryce.

"He's very thoughtful," she said as she smelled the roses.

"He likes you. He likes what you do to me."

She let out a laugh. "We haven't been around each other very much."

Jesse walked toward her and rested his hands on her hips. "It's not me being around you that has an effect on me. It's just you." He combed his fingers through her hair. "Love does crazy things to people."

Melissa swallowed hard. "Yes it does." Didn't she know that just standing in the bedroom with the man?

"I thought I was going to make it all the way till tonight without touching you." He moved in even closer, until she had to steady herself with her palms against his chest.

Jesse cupped the back of her neck and lowered his face until he was only a breath away. "I love you."

"Jesse…"

"You don't feel the same?"

The air caught in her lungs as she gazed into his gray eyes. She lifted her hand and brushed it over the sides of his hair, which laid flat today. She slid her fingers over his jaw and touched his lips. Her body trembled as she felt his breath on her fingertips. Every part of this trip was a gamble. It was a gamble to leave her son and her job. A gamble to be the woman on his arm and to face the criticism on the world. A gamble to want to tumble into bed with him and free herself from the worries of a single mother. But even more, she knew the biggest gamble rattled her heart and the words teetered on the tip of her tongue. "I do feel the same way." She felt her knees weaken. "Jesse, I love you too."

It was obviously all he needed to hear. His mouth came down on hers with a heated passion she hadn't felt in years. Urgency burned through their clothes as he lifted Melissa and she straddled him.

He held her tight, his mouth still on hers, and he began to walk out of the room.

"Where are you going?" She laughed through their kiss.

"My room."

Melissa lifted her head back. "That wasn't your room?"

"I didn't want to be presumptuous."

God, she did love this man. Who cared that there was nine years between them or that he was as beautiful as a god. She loved him. She absolutely loved him and she didn't think she could wrap herself around him any tighter to make him any closer.

As Jesse walked out to the hallway, he pressed her up against the wall. Her legs tightened around him as his tongue explored her mouth.

He moved his hands to the buttons of her shirt and nimbly began to unbutton each one.

There was a panic that surged through her when he parted the fabric. She didn't have nice lingerie. She had breast fed her son, her breasts were not taunt. But Jesse didn't seem to notice that as he pressed kisses over the swell of her breasts.

Parts of her reacted as they hadn't in years. Urgency, need, and desire all twisted inside of her.

Jesse gathered her back in his arms, her legs still wrapped around him and he carried her down the hall to his room and kicked the door closed behind him.

Chapter Thirteen

The room was silent—and bright. The midday sun was no match for the sheer curtains that hung from Jesse's windows.

He was afraid to move—afraid to speak.

Melissa had given herself to him, and in return, he'd been gentle, careful, and loving. Now she lay wrapped in his arms, breathing steady as though, perhaps, she'd dosed off for a moment. Then she turned in his arms. Her naked body pressed against his, and he pulled the sheet up around them.

Her new hairstyle was mussed and tangled. Her lips were swollen and her makeup smudged—and he'd never seen a woman more beautiful.

Jesse moved in and gently pressed his lips to hers. "Thank you for trusting me."

She only smiled and rested her head against his chest.

There was so much he wanted to say to her, but he knew it would all be for not. Melissa wasn't the kind of woman who did things without thinking them through. He was sure coming to California and sleeping with him was about the most reckless thing she'd ever done. But, in his head, it wasn't reckless.

This was forever, and that was exactly what he wanted. And Jesse Charles was used to getting what he wanted. But this was going to take work.

He wanted to marry Melissa.

He wanted to have her forever and make a family with her.

But she was level-headed—and she had a family. She had it all. A career she loved, a son, and a man who already took care of her. William Scott was more of a threat to him than he wanted to admit, and he wasn't even sure Melissa knew it.

Even his manager and that stupid model, who had claimed they were getting married, weren't as much of an obstacle as a man who truly loved a woman.

Jesse brushed his hand over her hair, and she looked up at him with those hazy brown eyes.

She smiled. "Your mother is going to know what we did."

"I'm not seventeen."

She nodded and rested her head against him again. She brushed the tips of her fingers through the small tuft of hair on his chest and then placed a kiss on his skin. "Thank you for being gentle with me."

"I don't want to scare you away."

"I'm not scared anymore." She shifted and looked up at him again. "I don't know how this will work. We come from such different places, but…" She lifted herself up onto her elbow and looked down at him. "I'm very willing to try, as long as I never have to move Jonah away from Aspen Creek."

Jesse rose up on his elbow to meet her. "I'd never ask you to do that." He ran his fingers through his hair. "In fact, I was thinking maybe I could buy your grandfather's land and…"

Melissa pressed her finger to his lips. "Shhhh. I'm not going to ask you to give up your life either." She lowered her hand. "I'm only going to ask you to be honest with me. Never lie to me."

"I wouldn't dare."

"If we're to be together—then it's you and me. You can't go on tour and come home to me if you find it necessary to have a girl after every show."

That made him sit right up. "I told you. I don't do that."

Melissa sat up, too. "I know what you said. I'm laying down my rules. I told you I loved you and that this whole different life and age difference can't matter."

"It doesn't."

"I'm going to be some old woman, and you'll still be a young man."

He chuckled. "Nine years. Not twenty. I will be right behind you as an old man when you're old."

She smiled. "Promise me we are exclusive and that I can trust you."

"You can trust me."

"That's all I need." She touched his face. "I love you."

The pain that had begun to form in his chest subsided. "I love you, too."

Melissa looked at his hair and then ran her fingers through it as if she were spiking it up. "What is the pattern for baldness in your family? Are you always going to look better than me?"

Jesse lowered her to the bed. "Impossible."

Melissa had thought she was nervous enough just being with Jesse, but now she was headed to Malibu to meet his mother.

Her foot tapped, and her hands shook. Jesse must have noticed when he reached for her hand and interlaced their fingers.

"Relax. I've never seen her bite someone."

Melissa nodded. "I'm sure there is a first time."

Jesse turned toward the beach and a row of houses that lined it. He pushed another button in his car, and one of the garage doors lifted.

"Your mother lives on the beach?"

"She has the very best of everything." His voice was flat, and Melissa decided she knew him well enough to understand that that meant he'd given her the best of everything.

He pulled into the garage, parked next to a red Mercedes, and turned off the engine as the door went down.

Melissa looked him over. His hair was now spiked, just as it was the night she'd met him—the blond tips freshly done. His dark glasses covered his eyes, and he'd changed into an embellished button-up shirt, which had gone unnoticed until now. This was a show to him, having to perform for his mother.

"You look nervous," she said to him.

"I shouldn't be."

"That's what you keep telling me."

Jesse turned to face her as he lifted his glasses to the top of his head. "Listen, I'm not an image of my mother." He shook his head. "What I mean is…who you meet is not what I am."

"You're not making sense."

He nodded. "My mother is materialistic. I'm not. Whatever she says today, understand one thing and one thing only." He focused on her. "I love you."

"I don't want to do this now." She tried to be humorous about it, but now it wasn't funny.

"It's a must if you're going to marry me some day."

He stepped out of the car, but Melissa sat there with the air stuck in her lungs.

Jesse opened the door and held his hand to her, but she didn't take it. She just sat there.

"Marry you?"

The sexy grin was back, and he looked at ease again. "I'm thinking big."

Melissa wasn't sure her legs were going to carry her into the house, but somehow she managed to climb from the car and take his hand.

Jesse led her into the house, which was small but very well decorated.

"I'll be right down," she heard a woman's voice call.

"Take your time," Jesse retorted.

Melissa looked around from where she stood. "Is this your trophy house?"

"You could say that."

The walls were lined with gold and platinum albums accompanied by his picture. The mantle above the fireplace was adorned with Grammys and other miscellaneous statues and trophies.

"I didn't realize you were *this* famous."

He tucked his fingers into the pockets of his jeans. "This isn't important to me. What I like is the music." He moved in closer to her. "She's into the fame and the recognition," he whispered. "That is why it's here and not on my walls."

She nodded as she heard the sound of someone coming down the stairs.

Jesse stood upright and walked toward his mother who greeted him with kisses on both cheeks and a very uncompassionate hug.

She was a small woman with blonde wavy hair, long red nails, and more jewelry on her arms and fingers than Melissa had ever owned in her life. She wore a sarong over a swim suit, sunglasses on her head, and jeweled sandals on her feet. The woman was something out of a movie, but not someone's mother.

Jesse took his mother's arm and walked toward Melissa.

"Christine, this is Melissa," he said using the woman's name instead of calling her Mom.

The woman held out her hand and shook the tips of Melissa's fingers. That was no handshake—in fact, she wasn't sure what she'd call that.

"Ms—Christine," she started as she realized she didn't know anything about this woman to call her anything but Christine. "It's nice to meet you."

Christine looked her over before turning her crimson lips into an obviously forced smile. "It's wonderful to meet you. Jesse has told me all about you."

Jesse moved in next to her and slid his arm around her waist. The flash of disgust in his mother's eyes was evident.

"You look like you were headed to the beach. Why don't Melissa and I let you to that."

"Oh, don't be silly. Jesse, why don't you go in and fetch that pitcher of lemonade Consuela made of us and bring it out to the porch."

Christine turned and walked toward the French doors that opened to the back patio. Jesse gave Melissa a nod to follow her, and he disappeared into the kitchen.

Melissa clasped her shaking hands together, blew out a deep breath, and followed Jesse's mother outside.

She had to admit, as she shut the door, that the view of the beach and the ocean was breathtaking. What a luxury to wake to such a sight, but then again, she'd never give up her majestic view of the mountains, even for a view of the ocean.

Christine sat down and slid on the pair of Chanel sunglasses.

"So, what is it you want with my son?" she asked as Melissa looked out over the ocean.

The tone of Christine's voice hadn't surprised her. After all, she was a mother. She'd question a woman's intention, too.

Melissa turned to face her. "I'm very fond of your son."

"You're having sex with him."

She was sure her face turned as red as Christine's nails. It had been obvious—they should have waited.

"I love your son."

"You and a million other women."

How was she supposed to respond to that?

Christine lifted her face to the sun. "He doesn't need some old lady with a kid. He's foolish to think he fell in love with some woman he saw from stage."

Melissa pushed back her shoulders. She wasn't one to fight with someone's mother, but... "My son adores him."

"Of course he does, dear." Christine lowered her chin. "My son is one of the most famous people in the world. You will ruin his image."

Melissa could feel the sting of tears in her eyes. But she refused to cry. This was what she'd expected from everyone. She told Jesse it was a mistake. This was proof.

Christine pulled her glasses off and her gray eyes, which matched Jesse's, bore into her. "My son is going to marry Noelle Camillo."

A lump lodged in Melissa's throat. She recognized the name from the newspaper article William had shown her.

Christine slid the sunglasses back on her face as Jesse opened the door and stepped through. Melissa turned away and looked out over the ocean. She heard him set the tray he'd carried down on the table.

"You know, Melissa and I have some things to do before the concert tomorrow. I hope you don't mind if we head out."

"Oh, I understand. You're such a busy man, darling. You have so much work to do."

Jesse rested his hands on Melissa's shoulders, and she turned around.

"It was nice to meet you, Christine."

Christine gave her a curt nod. "Likewise."

Jesse opened the door and led Melissa through the house and out to the car. He opened the door, and she slid into the seat.

"I'll be right back. I forgot something," Jesse said as he shut the door. He disappeared before she could ask what he'd forgotten.

A few moments later, he returned, climbed in beside her, and slammed his door. It was obvious what he'd forgotten inside—to tell his mother off in front of her. Well, in her book that made him a gentleman.

He drummed his fingers on the steering wheel before giving it a good hard smack.

Melissa flinched in her seat.

"I'm sorry," he said as he gripped the wheel.

"Maybe you should take me back, and I'll call a cab for the airport."

"You think I'm going to let her take control of this? Melissa, she's done that my whole life. I have a great life, don't get me wrong, but this isn't what I wanted. What child wants to give up their childhood so their mother can have every luxury she thinks she deserves?" He sucked in a breath. "I'd give all this up for you and Jonah."

"Don't put us in your family fights."

"You're not in my family fight—you're the family I would fight for."

Now the tears his mother had caused surfaced and rolled down her cheeks.

"Oh, I didn't mean to make you cry." He reached over and brushed away her tears. "I just won't have someone push you away from me. I love you."

"I love you too, but this isn't meant to be. She said you're getting married, too."

"I know what she said. I heard her." He sat back in his seat and raked his fingers through his hair. "How can I

---

convince you that I don't know Noelle Camillo? She's a client of my manager. He wanted to set us up. Publicity. I said no. That's not how I work, but it must have leaked."

"I can't do this, Jesse."

He pushed the button that opened the garage door and put the keys in the ignition.

"Don't give up on me."

Melissa wiped away her tears. "I won't."

"Good. So, you want to drive a convertible?"

That made her smile. "We didn't have much luck the last time I drove you anywhere."

"That depends on how you look at it. If I remember correctly, I got very lucky."

Heat rose in her cheeks, and she thought about how much further they would have gone if William hadn't shown up.

"Okay, I'll drive. Where are we headed?"

"How about a hot dog on Santa Monica Pier?"

She smiled at the chance to see another place she'd only seen in the movies.

"Oh, and Bryce got us courtside tickets to the Lakers tonight."

Her smile subsided. Courtside at a Lakers game meant cameras. The world was about to be introduced to Melissa Mathews—the plain-Jane, biology teacher girlfriend of Jesse Charles.

Chapter Fourteen

They'd dined on the pier and driven around town. Jesse had pointed out the tourist spots to Melissa on their way back to his house.

Now she stood in front of the mirror in his massive bathroom and looked at herself. She'd done her hair just as Emmy had shown her, and it was gorgeous. The makeup she'd chosen was subtle. She wore a designer pair of jeans she'd kept tucked away in her closet for the better part two years, her only pair of chunky heels, and a flowy cotton shirt. She thought she looked the part.

Jesse walked up behind her and wrapped his arms around her. He looked her over in the mirror.

"God, you're beautiful."

"I'm nervous."

Jesse placed a kiss on her neck. "Don't be. I don't care about the other people out there. I care about you."

He kissed her neck one more time and then looked at himself in the mirror. She knew he'd spent the previous hour primping. His hair was molded into the Jesse Charles signature blond spikes. The shirt he wore buttoned down the front and was embellished with design. The sleeves were short and tight around his sculpted biceps. Just below the cuff of his sleeve she noticed an arm band tattoo.

"Come here." She pulled him to her and examined the tattoo. "Why didn't I notice this before?"

"You had your eyes closed."

She nodded. "I guess I thought if I couldn't see my body then neither could you."

He moved in closer and placed his hands on her hips. "I know every inch of your body—from the freckle on the back of your neck to the scar on your stomach from Jonah."

She took a step back and looked down at the counter.

Jesse was quick. He was behind her with his arms wrapped around her waist again.

"Don't hide from me. I want to be the last man that knows every inch of you."

"I'm not as beautiful as you are."

"I'm expected to be. It sells. This isn't what I look like sitting on your couch."

Melissa nodded. She understood that, too.

Jesse turned her toward him, placed his finger under her chin, and lifted her face. "I think that scar is the most beautiful part of you. You gave life to Jonah. That's nothing to be ashamed over."

"It is when you're having sex with someone in their twenties."

His lips pursed. "I'm someone who loves you more than you can possibly understand." He sucked in a breath. "Marry me. Have a baby with me. Take me away from all this and make me a normal man."

Melissa moved out from him and out to the bedroom. He followed. Of course, he did. A look of anguish masked his beautiful face.

"Is that what you want from me? You want me to take *you* away from all this?" She waved her hands in the air to encompass their surroundings. "Are you using me?"

His eyes shot open wide. "No!" He moved to her in a quick, fluid motion. "I love you. Do you think I just throw that around? I would be honored to be your husband. I love your son. I would do anything to have him as mine. I wasn't kidding back there when I said marry me."

"Jesse, this is all crazy."

"I know." He cupped her face in his hands. "That's what makes it perfect."

He lowered his lips to hers and kissed her until she melted against him.

"Marry me," he whispered against her cheek.

"No." The word was mumbled against his mouth as he kissed her again.

Without pulling away, he deepened the kiss.

"Think about it."

She rested her head against his chest and sucked in a breath of courage. "I'll think about it."

Courtside at the Lakers game was exactly as Melissa had thought it would be. Just beyond them there were actors, politicians, singers, and a slew of other famous people vying for their spot with the publicity seeking public.

Jesse kept her close, his fingers intertwined with hers the entire time. When he could feel her tense, he'd whisper in her ear. He pointed out his guard, so she knew where her safe exit was, and he promised her it would be a night to remember.

Toward the end of the second quarter, Jesse's phone rang, and a bright, wide smile surfaced on his lips when he answered it.

"You can see us?" he asked. "She does look nice, doesn't she?" He listened to the voice on the other end and nodded his head. "Thanks for sharing her. I'm having a wonderful time. I'll see you soon, too. Here's your mom."

Jesse handed her the phone.

"Jonah?"

"Yeah, he saw us at the game."

Melissa put the phone to her ear and covered her other with her hand to block out the noise. "Jonah, why are you calling Jesse?"

"He gave me his number. And I saw you. You look nice."

Now she was smiling. "Thank you. Are you being good for Grandma?"

"Yeah. Hey, did you get me anything? Did you see the Hollywood sign? Did you go to the ocean?"

Melissa laughed. "I'll tell you all about it when I get home on Sunday. I love you."

"I love you, too. Tell Jesse I love him, too," Jonah said and the phone connection ended.

Melissa sat and stared at the phone.

"Is everything okay?"

She looked up at him. There were tears fighting to surface. "He says he loves you."

She handed him back his phone, and he tucked it into his pocket. "Great kid."

"Yeah." Melissa bit down on her lip. The sentiment had stirred her up, and her emotions were fighting for position.

Jesse took her hand again, and his thumb brushed against her skin as his attention diverted back to the game. Melissa's attention, however, was on her son's last words. She didn't throw those words around, and he certainly didn't either. Jesse meant something to Jonah. He meant something to her.

She'd be foolish to let a man—who, albeit, came from an entirely different world—walk out of her life when all he wanted was to love her and her son. And he'd been very sure of himself when he'd said he wanted to have a baby with her.

Why would he risk his entire career on her if he didn't really love her?

Why should she risk never loving again just because he was big city and she was small town? Didn't he say he'd give it all up for her?

She'd never expect him to, but…

At that moment, the crowd was on their feet. There was a foul on the court. Melissa's mind was spinning, and Jesse's hand gripped hers.

She looked up to see he had gotten to his feet. She still sat there, but she knew what she wanted.

When he sat back down, she leaned in close.

"I'll marry you," she whispered in his ear.

He turned. Those hypnotic gray eyes were wide, and a smile formed on his lips.

"Really?"

"Yes."

He gave her hand another squeeze. "Only because I want to tell Jonah first, I'm not going to gather you in my arms and make a scene. But know on the inside, I'm about to burst."

She smiled. His eyes told her that.

But he did lean in and gently press a kiss to her lips.

"You've made me very happy."

"I promise to always make you happy," she said as his arm came around her shoulders, and he pulled her in closer to him.

The sun was bright when Melissa finally pried open her eyes. It had been nearly three in the morning before she and Jesse had settled down to actually sleep in the bed they'd made love in for hours.

She rolled to gather him in her arms, only to find he was gone and a single rose was left in his place.

A smile formed on her lips as she picked up the rose and put it to her nose.

Melissa climbed out of the bed and found he'd left her with a robe and an enormous pair of slippers. She chuckled to herself as she slid them on and then went to the bathroom to tie up her hair.

She could smell food cooking from the kitchen, and she hurried down the steps to find Bryce donning an apron and stirring eggs.

He never turned around, but he'd noticed her. "Good morning, beautiful."

"Good morning."

"How'd ya sleep? Did you sleep?" He chuckled as he poured the eggs from the pan onto the plate.

"Yes, we finally slept."

Bryce carried the plates to the counter where Melissa took a seat.

"He's with his trainer."

She nodded. He could read her, too.

"So do you live here, too?" she finally asked as she took a fork full of eggs to her mouth. "Oh, this is good."

"I'm a wiz in the kitchen." He took his own bite. "I live in the guest house. My nephew is very good to me."

Melissa covered her mouth, but she couldn't wait to speak. "Nephew?"

"Yup. Mr. Sexy Pants is three years my senior and my nephew."

That explained the uncanny similarities. She narrowed her brows, and he grinned.

"You wanna know how that works, don't you?"

She only nodded.

"His mama's daddy and my daddy are the same guy. I never met him and she says he was an S.O.B., but that's that. He knocked up my mama and voila! Here I am."

Melissa absorbed the news he was giving her. She had never met a family of such dynamics before.

Bryce reached toward his leather book and pulled out a newspaper. He set it in front of her. "Looks like you made your first big splash, too."

Melissa picked up the paper and saw a picture of them kissing at the Lakers game. Oh, William was going to have a coronary over this one.

She read about the mystery woman Jesse was seen with, though it wasn't much of a mystery. The article stated that she was the very woman he'd pulled on stage in Grand Junction.

She wondered how long the photographer had been watching them. The story even talked about them sharing a phone call. Dear Lord, what if someone had heard their conversation?

There was no mention of that.

"Is this how his life goes? Every morning waking to see what someone wrote about him?"

Bryce nodded. "That's how it goes around here."

"How does he deal with this?"

"He hates it." He leaned in closer to her. "Wait till they hear about your wedding plans."

She dropped her fork. "He told you?"

Bryce just smiled and sat back in his chair. "No. I just figured. I can read you both like a book."

"You can't say anything."

"Honey, I'm not out to hurt him. I wouldn't do that."

"Do what?" Jesse asked as he walked through the door in a tank top and shorts and dripping in sweat.

He walked to Melissa and gently placed a kiss on her lips.

"You look beautiful this morning, my dear."

"Thank you."

He took her fork and a hefty bite of her eggs. "Why don't you cook this for me? That's good."

"She's prettier," Bryce retorted. "Besides, you're on concert day diet. Nothing good for you to eat."

Jesse laughed as he pulled open the refrigerator and pulled out a bottle of water. He held it to his forehead.

He nodded to the paper. "I see he's shown you the paper."

"I'm sorry if I caused you any embarrassment."

Jesse shook his head. "What would make you say that? I'm not embarrassed by you."

"This line *the very plain and aged woman to Jesse Charles's side.* That doesn't bother you?"

"Only because they think you're plain and aged. To me, you're absolutely perfect."

Bryce leaned in to her. "Damn, he is in love with you."

Jesse walked to her. "You can't read this crap. That's all it is—crap."

"This is what the world thinks of me."

"That's what one, small-minded person thought. I'm not going to lie. Three weeks ago the world thought I was marrying some model I don't know. I think now that they see the woman I am going to marry, things will be different. But they're going to throw it around first."

Melissa shoved the paper away. "I don't know what to do with it, in my heart."

"Nothing. You let it go." Jesse kissed her forehead. "I'm going to grab a shower. It's sunny. You should sit poolside and relax."

He ran off up the stairs, and Bryce covered Melissa's hand with his.

"Don't let this get to you. He's learned to let it slide, and if you're going to be his wife, you have to let it slide, too."

"I'm not built for this."

Bryce gave her hand a squeeze. "Oh, but I think you are." He stood and gathered their plates and dumped them into the sink. Then he took his leather book and held it to his chest. "I'll be back for you in two hours, and we have a shopping date. They thought you were a plain-Jane? Not after they see you tonight." He gave her a wink and left through the back door.

Melissa sat there a moment longer. She contemplated going upstairs and joining Jesse in the shower, but he seemed to have concert day rituals so she didn't want to bother him. Instead, she walked outside to the back patio and sat in a lounge chair by the pool.

She kicked her feet up and rested her head back, letting her skin soak up the sun. Okay, maybe the wife of a rich pop star wouldn't be too bad. She could certainly get used to swimming pools and sunshine in December.

The sun suddenly disappeared, and when Melissa opened her eyes, there was a man standing over her looking down at her in expensive sunglasses and an enormous Rolex on his arm.

"So you're her, huh?" The man sat down in the adjacent lounge seat and rested his arms on his knees as he looked her over. "He's really out to fuck this all up, isn't he?"

"I beg your pardon. And who are you?"

"I'm the one who is here to tell you to take a hike."

Melissa felt the heat rise in her cheeks, and she knew it wasn't the heat of the sun. She sat up and faced him.

"That didn't really answer my question."

"Tyson Brooks. Jesse's manager."

Melissa nodded as the man looked at his watch and then scanned a look over her. She realized this was the wrong time to have made an impression on him. Her hair was mussed from hours of sex and then sleeping in his client's arms. Her makeup was only remnants from the night before, and she was naked under Jesse's robe.

Tyson leaned in closer. "Do you think you're the only woman I've found lounging out here in the state?" He motioned to her robe. "Honey, you're a drop in the bucket."

Melissa swallowed hard. There were tears threatening to fall, but she refused.

"Go home. Be a hero in your Podunk town, but leave him alone."

This was a time to be the woman she was trained to be—a woman who defended her man.

"If Jesse asks me to leave, then I'll leave. But he's not going to ask me to do that. We have plans, and you're not going to stop them."

Tyson crossed his arms over his chest, and the sun reflected off the watch that had earlier caught her eye.

"What? He said he loves you? Wants to marry you?" He leaned back in. "Sweetheart, you're reeled in hook—line—sinker."

Her lips trembled, and the tears were almost surely going to fall now.

Tyson stood and looked down at her. "I meant it. Back your crap and go. He and Noelle are getting married. You're just a little bump in the road to bring in the publicity. Honey, you're nothing. Go home."

He started to the back door when it opened, and Jesse walked through.

"Tyson, what are you doing here?"

"Just having a word with your lady friend."

Melissa stood, but she couldn't look Jesse in the eyes. He reached for her and pulled her to him.

"She's not my lady friend. Melissa is my fiancée."

Tyson ran his tongue over his teeth and nodded. "Is that so? Well, congratulations then."

But there was something underlying in the conversation. Their eyes were intense on each other, and Melissa wondered how much of what Tyson had said was true.

Jesse looked down at her. "Sweetheart, why don't you go get ready for your shopping trip with Bryce. I need to have a few words with Tyson."

Melissa nodded and headed into the house. She didn't look back. She couldn't hear their words. But one thing was clear. Get ready, get packed, and get the hell out of L.A..

Chapter Fifteen

Melissa showered as quickly as she could. She'd surely miss having heated jets from every direction, but that's what vacation was all about, right? Just the amenities—and the broken hearts.

The tears were in full swing now. She ripped a comb through her hair, and her underlying curls sprung up. Who cared. No one in the man's life wanted her there—maybe even he didn't want her there.

She quickly pulled out a pair of pants and threw on a shirt. Then she went to packing as quickly as she could.

The door opened behind her, and Jesse walked through and slammed it.

He didn't say anything, but he paced. With his fingers, he combed through his hair and then he rubbed his palms together. This was fury building in a man she didn't know very well. Dear God, what was she doing here?

"You're packing?" He was curt and to the point.

"It seems best."

Jesse nodded and then moved in quickly and gripped her arms. The shock was enough to make her gasp, but she realized he wasn't hurting her.

"Don't go. Please don't let this get to you."

"Jesse, I don't belong here."

"One night. All I need is one night to say goodbye to everything and head home with you."

She shook her head and threw another blouse into her bag. "You can't do that in one night."

"Damn it, Melissa." He turned her toward him. "I love you, and you're letting these unimportant people fill your mind with lies."

"But I don't know what the truth is out here. I know my town. I know my people, my students, my life."

"I want to be part of that life. Please don't lock me out."

She let her shoulders drop. "I'm worth all of this to you?"

"Haven't I been trying to make that clear to you?" He moved in and wrapped his arms around her waist. "I love you. I want to marry you. I want Jonah as my son." He brushed his fingers through her curls. "I want a child of my own with you, maybe a house full."

"But all this…"

"Isn't important." He smiled. "Melissa, if I never sang another note I'd still be fine. I've written all my songs and have rights to the songs from the group. Other artists record my music, too. Don't you see? I don't have to sell out crowded arenas to do what I love to do. And I can do that from the sanctity of Aspen Creek."

"Your mom…"

"Will be fine without me here. I've set her up nice, and that's all she ever cared about."

"But she hates me."

"She's never liked anyone in her whole life. Don't take her opinions to heart."

"Tyson…"

"Will be fired." He shook his head. "He doesn't have my best interest at heart."

"Because he doesn't like me?"

"Well, that's only one reason. There are a million more."

Melissa leaned into him and rested her head on his chest. "You'll really move to Colorado?"

"I'd like to buy your grandfather's place and raise our family there."

He sure knew how to tug at her heart strings.

She chuckled. "Mom said someone was already looking at it and made a bid."

"I'll bet I could out bid them."

Melissa sighed. "I could pull some strings."

Jesse's arms came around her and held her tighter. "You'll stay. Maybe tonight I could even announce our engagement when I sing to you. God, wouldn't that piss Tyson off."

She lifted her head and looked up at him. "You'd better call my son first."

Jesse smiled. "He did give me permission to ask you. I guess I'd better let him know it all worked out."

"You asked his permission to marry me?" The tears were back, but at least happy tears didn't hurt.

"I'm a gentleman. If he had said no, I'd have let you pack." Jesse gave her a gentle kiss on the forehead. "I love him, Melissa. I have an amazing opportunity to be a good father to him, and with the understanding that I keep his father's memory alive for him."

Melissa sucked in a sob. Oh, this man and his words.

He took hold of her hands and kissed each one. "Let's go call him."

Jonah had been very matter-of-fact when they'd told him. He'd known that was where everything was leading the moment Jesse called his mom on stage. But his voice carried his excitement.

Her mother was cautious but equally as excited.

She'd wait until she got back to Aspen Creek to tell William. After all, that one wasn't going to go as well.

Jesse had left her for his last sound checks and whatever business he had to attend to before his final concert. Bryce had a car ready and waiting for them in the drive.

"We're taking a limo?" Melissa grabbed hold of his arm.

"Oh, honey. Why not live it up? Besides Jesse is footing the bill, and we are going to do some damage."

"I can't let him buy me clothes."

"Like hell you can't. If that man is going to be your husband, you'd better get used to having everything you want."

She sighed as the driver opened the door for them. "With him by my side, I'll have everything I need."

"I believe that, too." He patted her hand, and they climbed into the limo and headed down to Rodeo for some shopping.

Three hours later, with a bed full of shopping bags, Melissa fell into the chair in Jesse's bedroom, exhausted. For the first time in her life, she understood the term *shop till you drop*.

Bryce was a machine. He'd just look at something and know it would fit her and look perfect. And when she tried it on, he'd been right. Now the trick was going to be getting it all home, but Bryce had ensured her they'd ship it back to Colorado. That would be "easy peasy," he'd said.

The outfit she was to wear was hanging on the door to the closet. It was simple, a pair of jeans and a beautiful, silk blouse. The heels he'd chosen for her had her a bit nervous. Only a few weeks after a sprained ankle, she didn't think she should be walking in such unstable shoes. But she'd learned quickly that Bryce could talk anyone into anything.

A stylist was on her way up to her to do her makeup and fix her hair. She'd once looked forward to this, but that was prom and it involved her girlfriends. Now she was just a ball of nerves waiting to explode.

Melissa sucked in a breath and let it out.

If she was going to be Mrs. Jesse Charles, she was going to have to learn how to present to the public.

Another two hours later, Melissa walked out of the bedroom a new woman. She'd never felt so amazing in her entire life, and that included her wedding day.

As she descended the stairs, she noticed Jesse sitting on the couch in the formal sitting room. A smile had formed on his lips, and his eyes lit up when he saw her.

That alone had her heart doing flips in her chest. She loved this man more than she'd wanted to ever admit. This was going to be the strangest journey—a lifetime with a younger man who adored her. But it felt right. It felt real.

He stood and crossed to her. "I don't even have words for how amazing you look."

"You have a great team to put me together. "

"Oh, sweetheart, you don't need a team. This is all you."

He moved in and kissed her cheek so he wouldn't mess up her lipstick.

He took hold of her hands and ran his thumb over her knuckles. "I have a car outside waiting for us. I have to get there for wardrobe."

She nodded as he took her hand and led her out to the car that waited for them.

Melissa leaned into Jesse as he held her close. The traffic was heavy, but she'd learned quickly that it was the norm for L.A..

Bryce sat in the front seat with the driver, and the privacy screen had been raised between them.

Jesse maneuvered himself so he could kiss Melissa, which he did deeply and passionately.

"I love you."

She smiled. "I love you, too."

"So we've told your mom and Jonah that we're going to get married."

"We did."

"And Bryce, well, he already knew."

"Uncanny how he can read us."

Jesse laughed. "I told my mother today."

He was still smiling, but she could read his eyes. That hadn't been a happy moment. But she wasn't going to mention it. Her marriage to Jesse had nothing to do with the woman.

"Tonight I'm going to announce that I asked you to marry me, and I'm going to bring you out on stage and sing to you."

"Admirer?"

"Yes."

She nodded. "I think it's appropriate. You were a very unexpected admirer to me."

"Well, now I'll be an expected one because I will admire you until I die."

She rested her head on his shoulder. She liked the sound of that.

Jesse reached into his shirt pocket, and Melissa adjusted so she could see what he was doing.

Between his finger and his thumb, he pulled out a diamond ring. She gasped aloud.

"I picked this up for you today."

The tears were back, but they couldn't fall. No! Her makeup, but it was growing harder to hold them back.

Jesse took her hand and slid the ring on her finger.

"You'll still marry me?"

Melissa looked down at the solitaire diamond that had to be no less than two karats. She couldn't speak. She couldn't grunt. But somehow, while holding back the tears, she managed to nod her head.

"I was thinking a nice, private Christmas wedding in Colorado. What do you think?"

"I think that sounds very nice." Her voice cracked as she spoke.

Jesse wrapped her back into his arms. "We're going to be so happy. You. Me. Jonah. We will be the perfect, little family."

Nothing could diminish her happiness. Dear Lord, she begged, don't let anything ruin the bliss that is running through my veins.

The limo turned into the parking lot of the arena. The driver took them to a garage door where groups of people had already formed a mob. Some carried posters, others wore T-shirts bearing Jesse's face, and others just stood there screaming and crying, just as she'd seen in footage of Beetles concerts.

Security guards pushed back the crowd as the limo drove through and the door opened, allowing the car inside.

A moment later, the car came to a stop and the noise had died down. Other groups of people started for them, and each looked as though they had an agenda.

"This is it."

Melissa nodded.

"Stay with me at all times. Smile and just keep walking."

She nodded again, and he gave her a gentle kiss.

"They are going to notice the ring."

"Should I take it off?"

"Never." He smiled. "But just keep your head high and only go with Bryce, okay?"

"Okay."

"I love you."

She let out a deep breath. "I love you, too. Now let's make a splash."

"That's my girl."

The door opened and Jesse exited the limo, stopping to help Melissa out and hold tight to her hand.

Bryce was right next to her the moment she started walking.

He leaned in close and whispered, "Nice rock."

"Thank you very much."

"Very official."

"That it is."

"Good." He let his stride slow, but was always right behind them.

Agents from the arena started talking to Bryce and Jesse. Then a reporter snapped a picture and asked him questions which had nothing to do with the tour. Melissa just kept smiling.

It took nearly ten minutes to walk a few feet to the dressing room, but once inside, most of the crowd stayed out.

But there, in the room, was Tyson.

He smiled wide when Jesse walked through the door, and the moment he saw Melissa, his smile dipped into a scowl.

Bryce took hold of her arm and steered her toward the couch as Tyson moved in on Jesse.

Bryce retrieved them each a bottle of water and showed her where to sit.

"He'll be a bit. You doing okay?"

"Until I fall on my butt on stage tonight."

"You'll do fine." He gave her a nudge. "That S.O.B. is going to have a bad day tomorrow," he whispered again.

"Jesse said he was firing him."

"Yeah, he's shady."

Melissa could have told him that, but the man scared her to death. He might be shady, but it was hard not to believe everything he said.

Jesse was surrounded by different people for nearly an hour. Bryce had been pulled away as well, and Melissa sat alone on the sofa.

She couldn't help but wonder if Jesse would actually give up all of this attention just to live quietly with her. Could he?

This was his life.

She guessed she'd have to learn to trust more than she'd ever trusted before because she knew she couldn't travel with him always.

She loved him. It was all worth it—she continued to tell herself.

When the team of people who had surrounded Jesse all night finally left his side, he crossed the room to Melissa and held out his hand.

"Show time."

She took his hand and stood up next to him. "I think you look more beautiful than you said I do."

"Impossible." He kissed her on the cheek. His headset had already been taped against his cheek. "Bryce is going to show you where to stand. He'll send you out when it's time."

"Okay."

"Tonight, you sleep in my arms."

"Deal."

"Tomorrow I'm flying home with you."

She smiled. "I like that."

Just as they walked toward the stage, the crew was setting up his set. The opening act walked off the stage and gave Jesse a nod as they moved past.

She saw a mask nearly form on his face. A different man was walking away from her. It was an act, this man who performed on stage. The one who held her in his arms was the real thing—and all she could have ever asked for.

The concert was an hour in, and Admirer was to be the last song before the intermission. Her heart pounded in her chest. She was about to be announced as the woman he was going to marry, and she'd walk off stage with him, hand in hand.

Bryce had been called off, but she could see him and he'd call for her when it was time.

"He's very talented, isn't he?"

Melissa turned to see Tyson standing next to her, his sunglasses still on despite the dim sidelights backstage.

"Yes, he is."

Tyson stepped around her and then stood right in front of her. "He's not going to marry you."

"Yes. Yes he is." She held up her hand.

"Nice rock. He's a multimillionaire. He can buy those by the case."

Melissa felt her jaw clench.

Tyson stepped in. "You need to go now."

"I'm not leaving."

"You're only going to get hurt. If you don't want to see the destruction, run. He'll understand."

"I'm-not-going."

Tyson stepped to the side just far enough to let her see around him. What she saw was Noelle Camillo walking toward the curtain. The part that didn't go unnoticed was the tight dress that clung to her curves and the enlarged, round stomach which was so well pronounced.

The tears were back. How could she fight them now?

"The baby is Jesse's. He's already asked her to marry him."

The first tear fell.

"Now, there is a car waiting for you right through that door. A plane is waiting for you, and your luggage will be sent back to you."

Melissa watched as Noelle moved toward Bryce and Bryce looked for her, but Tyson was moving her out of his line of sight.

"You'll go now, or tomorrow's paper will have a picture of the two of you in a very compromising position. How will that go over in that small town of yours and that teaching position you hold so dear."

She couldn't let that happen. She couldn't even question him.

"Leave." He opened the door to the outside, and just as he'd said, a car waited for her.

What choice did she have?

She stepped toward the car, and the door to the arena slammed closed behind her.

Jesse was singing his heart out, but it was because he knew this was the end. The end of the tour—the end of an era.

Oh, it'd been fun, but he was moving on. Damn! By Christmas he'd be a father to a pre-teen. Okay, he had to clear his mind. That nearly caused him to miss a note.

The number was over, and the music and lighting changed. The tempo slowed, and the stage crew delivered two stools to center stage.

Cell phones and lighters illuminated and already the crowd was cheering, but he couldn't wait for the roar with his news. This was going to be the grandest moment in the history of Jesse Charles's concerts.

"We're going to take it down a bit." He wiped the sweat from his forehead. "This song is very special to me. See, I admire someone an awful lot. And we've made some plans."

Again, the crowd's approval was growing, and he hadn't even given them the news.

Jesse stood and started toward the side of the stage. "Yesterday I asked this beautiful woman to marry me, and she said yes. So now I'd like to bring her out here and introduce you to the future Mrs. Charles."

The arena erupted.

Jesse turned to see Melissa walk toward him, but instead a very pregnant Noelle Camillo was walking toward him.

The noise from the crowd pierced his ears.

Noelle sauntered toward him, cupped his face in her hands, and planted a long, wet kiss on his lips.

The crowd was eating it up.

Jesse gripped her hand and covered the mic on his cheek. "Where is Melissa?"

"Honey, she left." She took the hand that gripped her wrist and set it on her enlarged stomach. "She knows we're having a baby. She sends her best."

He wasn't sure how to leave twenty thousand people, but running out of the arena had crossed his mind.

Unfortunately, he was a showman and that meant the show must go on.

Chapter Sixteen

There had been only one choice when Melissa stepped foot onto that plane, which waited to take her back to her life, and that was to call William and ask him to be there when she arrived.

At least he hadn't disappointed her.

The moment she saw him standing there she'd run to him. She had wrapped her arms around his neck and held him.

William's arms came around her, and he let her stand there, in the middle of the airport, and cry on his shoulder.

"C'mon, let's get you home."

Melissa stumbled after him in the high heels that had now become too tight since her ankle had swollen on the plane.

Her body shivered. There was snow in Colorado, and she hadn't planned to be home and was unprepared.

William stripped off his coat and helped her into it.

"I'll go get the truck, and I'll pick you up."

She nodded as she wiped away the tears from her cheeks. He smiled and gave her a nod, then headed out into the fresh snow, with no coat, to get his truck.

The tears nearly froze to her skin as she stood there waiting, but there was no end to them. How had she been so foolish to think it was all true? It was just a joke to the rich and famous. Oh, she'd seen those shows and the movies where they took some average person and made them look famous. God, what a fool she was and how stupid she looked.

As she lifted her hand to wipe away more tears, the ring on her finger caught the light. She fisted her hand.

She'd send it back in the morning. Yes, that's what she'd do. Send back a two karat ring in a plain envelope. It would serve him right.

William pulled the truck up to the curb and hurried out to help her in. Once she was strapped in, he took her face in his hands.

"I'm glad you're home."

He shut the door and walked around to climb in the other side.

She braced herself for the barrage of questions and the *I told you so* to begin, but William focused on the road.

Not a single word was uttered between Grand Junction and the decent into Aspen Creek. That was when Melissa reached for William's hand and held it in hers.

"Thank you for coming for me," she said softly.

"I told you I'd always be here for you," he offered non-accusingly.

"He asked me to marry him." Another tear fell.

"I assumed that might have been the case by the rock on your finger."

She looked down at the ring. "Yes." She blew out a long breath. "What an idiot I was."

"No. You thought he loved you. You wouldn't agree to marry someone if you weren't in love."

She nodded, and now the tears turned to sobs. "I hate how this feels."

"You'll get over it. You're a strong woman."

This was why William had always been in her life. He knew her better than anyone.

Her cell phone rang in her purse, but she silenced it.

"Was that him?"

"I would assume so."

"You're not going to talk to him?"

She shook her head. "No. Never again."

William didn't say another word about the trip or the ring that adorned her finger. Melissa was thankful for his silence.

Her demeanor must have been less than grand when she returned to school because no one came to her to ask about the media coverage that had taken over the entertainment shows. But she'd heard the whispers, and she wondered when they would stop.

Now all she cared about was Christmas break and time to hide in her own home, away from the world. It would be enough time for everyone to forget that she was an idiot and had been used by a very powerful man. A very powerful man who had lied to her.

It would be just enough time for Jesse Charles and that woman to move on with their lives.

As the final bell of the day rang, Melissa dropped her head on her arms.

She heard the door close, and she looked up.

William stood there with a cup of coffee in his hand. "I thought you could use some. Your mom said she was picking up Jonah so you could stay and catch up."

She wanted to be gracious, but it was hard. However, she managed to smile and reached for the cup as he crossed the room.

"Thank you."

"Hard couple days?"

"I just want holiday break to get here, and I want to hide in my house."

William sat on the edge of her desk. "I wanted to take you to find a new car."

"I guess I need to do that."

"What about his truck? What are you going to do with that?"

Melissa was going to be civil when she spoke about him, but in her head, she was thinking of pushing the truck off a cliff.

"As soon as I have something to drive, I'll call Bryce and make him send someone for it."

"How about tomorrow after school? There was a lot in Grand Junction that had some nice options."

She nodded. At least William would keep his promises to always take care of her.

As he left her room, Emmy walked in, or rather snuck in, as Melissa didn't even realize she'd been standing there until she made some kind of noise.

"Hello, Emmy."

"Hi." She moved further into the room, her hands twisted around each other. "I just wanted to see how you were doing. I know everyone is staying their distance, but that just isn't my style. I also know I knew more than everyone, and I just wanted to make sure you were okay. Are you okay?"

The tiny, petite woman must have an amazing set of lungs, Melissa thought. She could run sentences on for days.

"I'm fine. I feel a little foolish, but I'm fine. Nothing a holiday break won't fix."

Emmy nodded. "Have you talked to him?"

Melissa shook her head. "Nope. I find no need."

"I read that…"

"Emmy, it's over. I was the biggest idiot to ever walk the earth. Now I look like a fool."

"No, you look brokenhearted."

And didn't she feel it, too?

Emmy started to step back, as though to retreat. "Well, if you need anything, you just let me know. I'm a good ear and a great secret keeper. By the way, your hair still looks great, and it did in the papers and at the Lakers game, too." She was almost to the door. "I'm heading into town. I have to mail off a piece of artwork for a contest. I don't know why I do that. I never win, but maybe someday, right?"

"You're going to the post office?"

"Yes."

Melissa looked down at her bag at the small box she'd wrapped up. Even Melissa had too much of a heart than to send the ring back in the envelope she'd originally thought of.

She picked up the box and walked toward Emmy. "Will you just hand this over? It's all ready. I calculated the postage online."

"You're sending him a gift?" she asked as she looked down at the name.

"No. Trust me. It's no gift. I'm giving him back a burden."

Emmy's brows narrowed and she nodded, but left with the very expensive ring in the box. Melissa wondered if it would ever make it to him. Then she thought about it and decided she really didn't care.

As promised, the next day William met Melissa at her house after school to pick her up. She parked the truck at the curb and not in the driveway, hoping that the phone call she'd placed during her lunch break would result in Bryce getting someone to come for the truck.

She was grateful to have had it, but she didn't need a daily reminder of how stupid she was.

William drove to the lot in Grand Junction where he'd scoped out a few cars. He thought an Acadia would be a great choice for her with all-wheel drive and yet it wasn't a monster of a truck, like the one she'd parked out in the street.

The salesman showed her nearly every car on the lot, but Melissa's head just wasn't into it. She didn't care about cars. She didn't care about safety and mileage. What she cared about was that stupid song was playing in the background and that no one but her could hear it. Jesse's voice was still in her head. It was still in her heart, and she hated that it affected her.

"Melissa, what do you think?" William asked, snapping her out of her mindless wandering of the lot.

"I think I want to go home."

The salesman was inching back, pretending as if he was checking on the car or a smudge on the paint.

William stepped closer to her. "You need a car."

"I need everyone to stop tiptoeing around me."

"You made a mistake. We all make them."

"And were any of your mistakes on Entertainment Tonight?"

He rubbed his hand over his forehead. "Let's just get you a car. Let's get home, and we can talk about what we're going to do now."

"We're? When did this become our issue?"

"When you left to sleep with the man and I told you I was in love with you."

That had the salesman excusing himself and high-tailing it into the office.

"So, this is what you'd expected?"

"Of course it was." He moved in closer. "C'mon, he's a nice kid, but he's a kid. What does he know about a family and a stepson?"

"You don't know him."

"And now you're defending him?"

She was, and she didn't know why.

Her ankle was aching in the cold. Her heart was breaking in her chest. And she just wanted to go home and lock herself in her bedroom again.

William reached his hand to her cheek. "Don't mourn this forever. This isn't what you had with Martin."

But it was and only she knew it. Even if it might have only been a month in the works, she'd loved the man and she had wanted to marry him.

William moved in closer. "Listen. This is really bad timing, but I think I should put it out there." He took a deep breath, and it hung in the frozen air. "I know you could never love me as you did Martin, but I would like to be your husband and a father to Jonah. Would you consider that?"

Melissa stood there, freezing, with her mouth hanging open. That had to have been the worst marriage proposal she'd ever heard. And worse yet, she was so depressed she was considering it.

Well, not yet. She wanted to be pissed just a little longer, and she was very pissed with William Scott for even moving in like that.

"Find me a damn car and tell me where to sign the papers. I don't even care if I have to pedal it."

She moved around him and walked back to the car.

Melissa ended up with the white Acadia William had seen when he'd gone to Grand Junction to pick her up from the airport.

It was a good car. She was pleased he'd put up with her long enough to get the papers signed.

As she parked the new car in her driveway the next day after school, she noticed the pickup truck was gone. A part of her was thrilled to not have the reminder sitting there taunting her. The other part ached—he was gone.

Melissa walked through the front door just in time to see Jonah run down the hall and slam his door. Melissa's mother followed until she saw her standing in the doorway.

"What happened to Jonah?" she asked.

"He got into a fight at school."

Melissa set her bag down on the floor. "He got into a fight? He's never been in a fight before."

"He's never had anything to fight over."

Melissa didn't like where this was going. "Jesse?"

"Yes."

She dropped her shoulders and went to his room. She knocked, but Jesse's voice had been cranked up on the speakers so she entered.

Seeing the face of the man she'd loved on her son's walls hurt nearly as bad as seeing her son crying. Melissa shut the door and sat down on the bed next to him.

"I hear you were fighting."

"Doug said Jesse is an idiot who got that model pregnant and was just using you to hide it."

She figured Doug had a good head on his shoulders, but she certainly couldn't tell her son that. "Jesse made a mistake."

Jonah's head popped up. "No. No he didn't. He doesn't know that woman."

"She was there, Jonah. The whole world heard him announce her as his fiancée."

"No, that was you. He was set up."

Melissa gritted her teeth. "How do you know that?"

"He told me."

"I don't want you talking to him."

"You can't stop me."

"I most certainly can. I'm your mother."

Jonah folded his arms over his chest. "Why did you leave? Why didn't you fight for him? He loves you, and you walked away from him."

"You can't sit here and tell me I hurt his feelings. I made a mistake. I fell in love with someone I really didn't know."

"But you did know him. You knew him better than anyone. No one wants him for who he is. They want the famous guy. Well, I want Jesse."

She took a breath to speak, but nothing came out.

They'd both lost.

She and Jonah had both loved him for different reasons. Time would heal everything. Everything would be okay.

Her mother was standing in the hallway when she shut Jonah's door behind her. Jesse's voice still echoed down the hall.

"Is he okay?"

Melissa nodded. "His heart is broken."

"Why don't you just call Jesse and sort this out."

She shook her head, surprised that her mother would even have suggested it. "No. I can't go back to that." Melissa started for her room. She turned back to her mother. "I see someone came for the truck?"

"Yes."

"Bryce?" she asked, sorry she'd missed him.

"No. A nice, young man." Her mother rested her hands on her hips. "If you won't talk to Jesse, what are you going to do now?"

"William wants to marry me."

Her mother let her hands drop to her sides. "He waits until now to share this with you?"

"He was letting me feel out this Jesse thing."

"This Jesse thing?" She walked to her and placed her hands on Melissa's shoulders. "You love Jesse. You agreed to marry him. Was that all a joke to you?"

"No. It was a joke to him."

"That's not what I'm hearing."

Melissa took her mother's hands. "Well, I'm not listening. I don't want to see his face, hear his name, or his voice." She nodded to Jonah's room. "In time, no one will remember me and Jesse. And," she said as she sucked in a painful breath that burned her lungs, "I'm going to marry William."

Chapter Seventeen

Melissa had left her mother standing stunned and silent in the hallway when she'd told her she'd planned to marry William. She figured, as they sat at the table for dinner, her mother was only getting even when she said she too had an announcement.

"I took an offer on Grandpa's land."

Melissa nearly dropped her fork on the floor. "You what? You didn't even talk to me about it."

"You seem to have your issues lately."

Melissa could feel the heat rise in her cheeks. "Who did you sell it to?"

"A man. What does it matter? We can't afford to keep it."

"Did you get a decent price?"

"Fair enough."

"Mom, you should have told me someone was interested."

"I did tell you. Before you left for California. Now I'm telling you I sold it."

Melissa's head was certainly going to explode. How could people take this much stress? Everything that had been normal and calm in her life was now a mess.

"Don't you have something you'd like to tell your son?" her mother asked. Now Melissa was sure she was going to die in that chair.

Jonah hadn't looked at her in days. He hadn't said much to her either. This was certainly wasn't going to make things better between them.

"William asked me to marry him," she said as Jonah peered at her through his bangs, which had gotten much too long. She tried to smile. "I've decided to marry him."

"I hate you!" Jonah was up from the table and down the hall, again slamming his door.

Melissa sat there, alone with her mother. She couldn't go to him. He deserved to be mad. She was mad, too.

She cleaned up the dinner table, and her mother headed out to her book club. Melissa decided on a nice, hot bath to ease the tension that had built up in her body.

As she passed Jonah's room, she could hear his voice. No doubt she was being ratted out to a friend. He deserved his allies. She wished, at that moment, that she had an ally of her own.

Only a week to go until Christmas, Melissa's students weren't the only ones not able to focus. She could care less about teaching.

It wasn't until after school William walked into her classroom, when no one was around, and wrapped his arms around her waist.

"I've waited all day to get near you. This part just might kill me."

Melissa rested her hands on his shoulders. "This still probably isn't a good idea. Not here."

He nodded and let his hands fall. As he tucked his fingers into the pockets of his suit coat, he rocked back on his heels.

"So I assume a quiet wedding is in order? You and me and maybe our families?"

"Yes," she said as she filled her bag with papers to grade. "I think that would be best."

William nodded. "I was thinking maybe Christmas Eve?"

Melissa swallowed hard. "That's kinda soon, don't you think?"

"Not for me. I've been waiting since I was seventeen."

She smiled, and she truly hoped it didn't look as forced as it felt. "I suppose that would be as good a time as any."

Snow had moved into Aspen Creek. Melissa hadn't been in much of a mood to decorate Christmas trees or bake cookies, but Jonah was. She realized she was stealing his holiday by being such a Grinch.

They'd gone up to her grandfather's land, for the very last time, and found the perfect Christmas tree. As William secured it into the bed of his truck, and Jonah and her mother climbed inside, she stood there staring at the home she'd always loved.

William walked up behind her and placed his hands on her shoulders. "It'll always be here. I'm sure you could come and visit."

She shook her head. "It won't be the same."

He turned her toward him. "Maybe someday we can buy a home and some land. Just ours. Who knows, maybe we'll have a house full of kids of our own." He pressed a gentle kiss to her lips.

"I think they're ready to go," Melissa said as she motioned to the truck.

"You know, we haven't even discussed a honeymoon."

Her chest hurt from the pain caused by thinking of what she was doing to her son, but it was the right choice. William was a good man. "Maybe we can think about that for the spring or summer."

"That would be a great idea."

The tree had finally been set up, and Jonah worked to sort the ornaments, as he did every year, while Melissa sat on the couch with a cup of coffee and William's arm draped over her shoulder.

Christmas music played on the radio as her mother sat in her chair knitting a new hat.

"Mom, I think we need some new ornaments. I think some of these are broken."

She laughed. "No, you just didn't like your glitter job in kindergarten."

Jonah growled and hung up the star made of Popsicle sticks.

The music changed, and White Christmas filled her ears. But this time, the voice wasn't that of Bing Crosby. It was a more familiar voice. One she'd heard sigh in her ear, call her name, and whisper *I love you.*

Tears began to form, but she pushed them away. She was bigger than this. She could control it.

Melissa lifted her coffee to her lips and sipped as all eyes were on her. William's hand gave her shoulder a squeeze. In another week, she'd be William's wife, and Jesse could go on with his life, his woman, his child.

Four days before her wedding to William, Melissa decided she'd better find some kind of dress. Just a cocktail dress from her closet wasn't going to do. He'd been patient and kind. He, at least, deserved for her to look her best.

She hated going into the stores, especially in the small town, and having everyone whisper behind her back. She'd towed the line her whole life, and now she was fodder for gossip.

Melissa knew, from living in the same small town her entire life, the gossip would die. Someday they'd all forget the handsome, young, sexy man who had come along and swept her off her feet. She and William would be just another couple, raising a son, living a quiet life in Aspen Creek.

But it was hard to escape.

As she checked out with a dress that would do, Jesse's song serenaded her on the speakers in the store. A new dress also meant a stop at the drug store to pick up some new stockings and a necessary new tube of mascara. It was nearly impossible to leave the store without reading any of the magazines on the stand. But each of them had Jesse's face so she just turned away.

As she walked out of the drug store, she thought perhaps a nice cup of coffee would be in order.

The store was full, more than usual, but she figured that was holiday traffic, even in a small town. As she placed her order and stepped to the side, the notifications on her cell phone rang. She looked down at her cell phone as a man passed by and opened the door.

His cologne caught her attention. It was Jesse's cologne.

It was instinct to look up, but the man was walking out just as she did so. A black leather jacket. Designer jeans. Spiky, blond hair.

Her heart began to beat so fast she thought it might escape her chest. She took a step toward the door to look at the man just at the moment Molly called her name for her coffee.

Melissa grabbed her coffee and headed for the door. A group of teenagers walked through the door. Each of them said hello to her, but she couldn't get past them fast enough.

When she made it outside, the man was gone.

The snow fell around her as the sun began to tuck itself behind the mountain. Obviously the holidays and her pending wedding were making her lose her mind.

Dinner that night was quiet, though William tried his best to ease the tension between him and Jonah. They talked about scouting adventures they had enjoyed and planned a sledding weekend.

Melissa's mother passed the basket of bread around the table. "So, did you find a dress?"

"Yes."

"It was busy in town."

Melissa looked at her mother. "You were in town?"

"Yes, we closed on the sale today."

Melissa set her fork down and wiped her mouth with the napkin she'd had in her lap. "Why didn't you tell me? I would have gone with you? I don't like that you've tended to this whole sale alone."

"I'm a grown woman. I can take care of business just as well as you can."

Melissa gripped the napkin in her hand. "I didn't mean to be disrespectful."

"Then don't be."

The tension, which William had worked so hard to erase, was growing thick again. That was when Melissa noticed the green on Jonah's hand.

"What did you get into?"

Jonah's eyes opened wide, and he exchanged glances with his grandmother. "I must have gotten into some paint."

Melissa's mother handed him another napkin to wipe at it. "There must have been a wet wall downtown."

"Jonah, it's in your hair."

He reached for it. "Oh, wow."

Melissa's mother buttered the bread she had taken from the basket. "It'll wash out."

William helped clean up dinner and sat with Melissa on the couch after everyone had gone to bed.

He wrapped his arm around her, holding her close. In time, she knew his closeness would be a comfort. In time, she'd love him more than a friend. In time, she would forget the pain of losing another man she loved.

"What do you think if I stay tonight?" William asked softly in her ear.

She knew it was obvious that her body tensed. "I think we should wait."

He let out a breath. "I understand."

"Jonah…"

"I know. I suppose it's different because it's me."

She knew he'd meant to stab her with his words just enough to make her wince. It had worked. But it wasn't worth delving further into what he'd meant. Yes, she went to California for a weekend with a man she barely knew. They'd had sex. They'd made plans. They'd said *I love you.*

She'd done none of that with William, and he'd been there for her since they were teenagers. She contemplated taking his face in her hands and kissing him, but she couldn't do it.

"Well, I suppose I should go. I told my mother I'd try to stop by." He stood and pulled her to her feet. "She's very excited to have you as a daughter-in-law. She always thought of you that way."

"That's very sweet."

He walked to the door and pulled his coat off the coat rack. He slid it on and looked down at her.

Cupping his hands around her face, he moved in closer. "You've made me so happy. I can't wait until Christmas Eve."

He leaned in and pressed his lips to hers.

It was now or never to seize the moment. Melissa lifted her arms around his neck and deepened the kiss.

A moan escaped him as he stumbled closer, gripping her waist.

When she finally pulled back and they rested their foreheads together, she wondered if he'd felt it too. She'd expected at least a spark—something that would ignite between them forever. But it wasn't there. She did love this man, but as a brother, a dear friend.

She searched his eyes. It was there, but he didn't dare say anything.

"Good night, Melissa. I love you. I'll see you tomorrow."

William walked out the door, and Melissa closed it and then leaned against it. She'd hoped the kiss would rock her world, just as Jesse's had. She missed his hypnotic eyes, his soft voice, his touch, his scent—damn it, she missed him.

As she walked past Jonah's room, she could hear the soft mumble of his radio. She wanted to go in and hold him. Not to comfort him, but to comfort herself.

She undressed and slid on her favorite pajamas. It was then she wondered if her luggage would ever arrive from California. Tyson had said they'd send it, but then again, why should she have ever trusted anything he'd said.

Melissa picked up her brush and pulled it through her hair. She walked toward the bed, but the picture of her and Martin caught her eye.

"Oh, Martin, I miss you. How could things have become so complicated?"

If only that one moment in time hadn't happened. Nothing would be different. Perhaps she'd have more children. Jesse Charles would have been someone in passing, regardless of whether he'd called her on stage. And William Scott would still be her friend.

"Too late now."

She took the picture and laid it down so that her own eyes were not watching her—judging her.

Chapter Eighteen

The ground had a fresh covering of snow, and it sparkled up at Melissa as she looked out her bedroom window on her wedding day.

She looked in the mirror. Her eyes had dark circles under them from not sleeping well.

How was she supposed to sleep? Never in her life had she been so nervous. In only three hours she would marry her dearest friend, but her heart ached.

She drew a hot bath and added soothing oils. It was a day to rejoice that someone loved her. It was Christmas Eve, what a joyous day. Happiness would fill her heart. She just had to let it in.

Melissa styled her hair and put on her makeup. Then she slipped into the pale dress she had chosen to marry William in.

She blew out a long breath as she looked at herself in the mirror. The time had come to move on.

The doorbell rang, and she knew there was no backing out. In an hour she'd be Mrs. Scott—if only it brought the same thrill to her heart as the thought of being Mrs. Charles.

Melissa took her necklace from her jewelry box and carried it out to the other room where William and her mother stood, dressed and ready for the wedding.

Jonah lay on the floor in his pajamas, watching TV.

Melissa greeted William with a gentle kiss and then handed him the necklace. "Can you help me with this?"

"My pleasure," he said as he clasped the necklace and kissed the back of her neck.

"Thank you." She smiled and turned to Jonah. "Jonah, why aren't you ready?"

"I'm not going."

"Sweetheart, we have an appointment. Go put your clothes on and let's go."

He stayed on the floor, his eyes glued to the TV.

Melissa walked toward him. "Jonah, this isn't the time to be stubborn. I'm getting married in an hour."

Finally he stood and faced her. "You're marrying him." He pointed to William. "But someone else asked you to marry him."

"Jonah, this is done. Get ready."

"No. Not until you admit you loved him."

Melissa gritted her teeth as the heat rose in her cheeks. "I did love him. He lied to me."

"He did not. You never gave him the chance to tell you his side."

William walked toward them, but Melissa shrugged off his approach.

"You have more paint in your hair."

"Who cares."

"I care. Go get ready."

The program he'd been watching flashed a picture of Jesse's face. It caught her attention.

"Jonah, turn that off."

"No." He turned up the volume.

"I said…" but the report had her stopping her demands. She shouldn't watch it. It was an entertainment show—there was nothing news worthy there. But now the volume was nearly deafening.

"So, where has Jesse Charles gone? Those planning the New Year's Eve concert in L.A. are asking the same thing," the woman on the TV announced.

Melissa moved closer, and Jonah reached for her hand.

"After yesterday's news that Noelle Camillo admitted to fraudulently naming Jesse Charles as the father of her child, the pop star has disappeared. Sources close to the singer say he has taken on some new scenery and might be hiding somewhere in the Colorado mountains."

Melissa covered her mouth with her hand. It had been a lie. The woman had lied. Jesse had been telling her the truth. She looked down at Jonah who smiled up at her as if he'd always believed in Jesse's innocence.

But it was when she looked at William, everything changed.

His eyes softened, and he took her face in his hands.

"I would have loved to have been your husband."

The first tear rolled down her cheek.

William brushed it away. "I know I can never make you as happy as he does. Go."

Melissa got into her new car and drove. She didn't have to think about where she was going. She knew right where Jesse Charles had fled to.

The snow on the roads made it nearly impossible to get up the mountain fast enough. It wasn't until she'd slid toward the guard rail that she knew she was going much too fast.

But she had to get to him. She had to know the truth.

When she turned the corner and drove through the open gate of her grandfather's ranch, there was the familiar pickup truck Jesse had bought to keep in Aspen Creek.

Damn, even her mother could keep a straight face. *Some young man picked it up.*

But as she turned off the engine and hurried up the stairs, anger began to take over the bliss that fueled her body. Why hadn't he just shown up and told her it was a lie? Why call her so she could ignore him? Why—why not come after her?

She reached for the door, narrowly missing the hole in the porch, and pushed her way inside.

A fire crackled in the fireplace. Two mugs sat on the old chest that was used for a coffee table, and the smell of cider filled the air.

"You know, that's trespassing," the familiar voice said, and Melissa turned to see Jesse standing in the doorway to the kitchen. He looked rugged and that made him even sexier than he'd been when he was wrapped around her—skin on skin.

"You can't be here."

"Oh, yes I can." His voice was low, and it sent a shiver down her spine.

"You can't live here."

"I have papers that say otherwise. Your mother signed them."

The tears were welling in her eyes. "You were the buyer?"

He took a step toward her. "From the very first call I made after I saw this place."

"I'll give you your money back."

"Nope." He walked closer.

"Are you wearing cowboy boots?" She hiccupped through her tears.

"Like 'em? These ones are for taking the ladies dancing. I have a trusty pair of work boots, too. And a nice Carhartt coat to keep me warm."

She looked up at him as he neared. His mouth was cocked into that grin which had won her over in the beginning. "You're going to go dancing?"

"I hear there's a wedding." He took another step until he was right in front of her. He touched the neckline of her dress. "This your wedding dress?"

"Yes."

"You look beautiful."

Her lip quivered as the first round of tears rolled down her cheeks. "You're not the father of her baby?"

"I told you. I didn't know her. She and Tyson worked that out. The baby is his."

"Oh," she said as she sucked in a breath. "I thought Tyson was married."

"He is—was. He's infamous for his publicity stunts."

She nodded, trying to understand the people in a life that wasn't meant for her.

"So, where is your husband?"

"My what—oh, I didn't get married."

"Too bad." He lifted his hand to her hair and brushed it from her face. "You make a beautiful bride."

"Jesse…" His name was only a whisper as he leaned his face to hers and took her mouth with his own.

His lips took possession of hers, his tongue explored, and the heat rose in her core. She wrapped her arms around his neck as he pulled her in closer. This was a kiss. The way her head swam, the rapid beat of her heart, the mindless whisper of *I love you* in her ear.

"I missed you," she panted as he broke the kiss and held her close.

"You never should have left. I turned to tell the world I was marrying you and that woman walked out on stage."

"I didn't know." She wept against his chest. "I didn't know."

"We're here now. Together."

She looked up at him, and he brushed away the few stray tears that had rolled down her cheek.

Then his eyes darkened with seriousness. "William."

"He sent me to you."

He gathered her up in his arms again. "I owe him one."

They both did.

"I need to call Jonah," she said as her mind finally cleared from the kiss he'd planted on her.

"He knows. C'mon, let me show you something."

Jesse took her by the hand and led her up the steps. As they turned the corner, the bedroom door to her grandparent's room was closed. However, the door to the room at the end of the hall was open. She moved past him. Something had caught her eye.

When she turned on the light, the room was filled with items that had been in Jonah's bedroom. The posters that had hung on his wall were now on the walls in this room. The green—the same green which had been in his hair and on his clothes—was painted on the walls.

"Jonah was here." Anger rose in her voice. "Why was my son here?"

"Because your mother brought him."

She looked back into the room. "I don't understand."

"Call it extreme wishful thinking on all of our parts. He painted the room the color he wanted it." Jesse moved next to her and slid his arm around her waist. "If, in the end, I couldn't convince you that I was telling the truth, or if I'd missed out and you'd married William, the house would have been yours."

She turned to him. "You would have done that for me?"

"It was the least I could do for you." He gathered her hands in his. "You don't understand. You gave me so much, even in our short amount of time. I've never wanted to be with someone so much. I've never loved anyone as much as I love you. When you left, I was broken."

"So was I."

Jesse combed his fingers through her hair. "So, you're not going to marry William?"

She smiled as she shook her head. "No. I love him very much, but only as the dearest friend I have."

"I can accept that." He kissed her fingers. "I have something else I want to show you."

He led her to the bedroom that had been her grandparents'. He opened the door and let her walk in.

The entire room had been remodeled, but the original bed and dresser, which her grandfather had made, still stood in the room.

There were drapes on the windows, a new duvet on the bed, and tiny pillows with roses.

"Oh, this is beautiful," she said, taking in the sight of it including a vase of roses on the nightstand.

"Bryce had a lot of fun with this room."

Melissa turned to face him. "Bryce. He was here? He was in town?"

Jesse laughed. "Yes. You almost caught him. I told him not to go into town, but he couldn't do without his special coffee."

She sighed. "He had on your cologne."

"He's kind of a thief."

She turned and looked at the room again. She couldn't have designed it better herself. It was amazing.

"Take a look at the pillows."

Melissa walked toward the bed and gasped when she saw the ring tied to the small pillow on the bed. "My ring. You got it back."

"Sorta chancy that it would make it, wasn't it?"

"That was kinda my point." She narrowed her gaze. "Sorry."

"I would have thrown it in the ocean if I couldn't get you back."

Jesse untied the ring from the pillow, took her hand, and held the ring at the edge of her finger. "Melissa, will you still marry me? And live in this little town with me? And share this amazing house with me and Jonah?"

The tears were back, but they were happy now. The joy of the moment coursed through her. She couldn't answer. All she could do was nod as he slid the ring back on her finger and then pulled her in and embraced her.

"You've made me very happy. It was worth giving it all up."

She stepped back. "You gave it all up?"

"Well, Bryce has a nice, new house, and I have a song writing gig."

"Well, as long as you're happy."

"Almost." He took her by the hand and led her to the last bedroom. He pushed open the door, and she stepped inside.

"A nursery?"

Jesse stood behind her and wrapped his arms around her. "This is the last part. The woman of my dreams. The home of my dreams. A son. The only thing missing is…"

"A daughter?"

"Only if she were just like you."

"You'd have your hands full." She turned to him. "Maybe a son to play baseball with."

"Now there is a fine idea."

"I'm sorry I left."

"I would never lie to you. You and Jonah are my world. I didn't know so much was missing from my life until you happened into it."

"It was quite unexpected."

He pulled her in tighter. "Secret admirers are nice, but unexpected admirers are even better."

"You know…" She took his hand and started pulling him toward the bedroom. "I have a funny feeling my mother and *our son* are on their way up here."

Jesse smiled wide. "You might be right."

"So that only gives us a few moments to get to work on your next task. Filling that nursery."

"If you insist."

"I absolutely insist."

Join me again in
Aspen Creek
in
September 2013
for the next book in the Aspen Creek Series
On Thin Ice

Meet the Author

Bernadette Marie has been an avid writer since the early age of 13, when she'd fill notebook after notebook with stories that she'd share with her friends. Her journey into novel writing started the summer before eighth grade when her father gave her an old typewriter. At all times of the day and night you would find her on the back porch penning her first work, which she would continue to write for the next 22 years.

In 2007—after marriage, filling her chronic entrepreneurial needs, and having five children—Bernadette began to write seriously with the goal of being published. That year she wrote 12 books. In 2009 the published author was born. In 2011 she opened her own publishing house, 5 Prince Publishing, and has released her own contemporary titles as well as the titles of many other talented authors..

In 2012 Bernadette Marie found herself on the bestsellers lists among her literary idols.
Bernadette is a hockey mom and herself a second degree black belt in Tang Soo Do.

She loves to meet readers who enjoy reading contemporary romances and she always promises Happily Ever After.

www.bernadettemarie.com
www.facebook.com/authorbernadettemarie
www.authorbernadettemarie.blogspot.com
@writesromance on Twitter
info@bernadettemarie.com

www.ingramcontent.com/pod-product-compliance
Lightning Source LLC
Chambersburg PA
CBHW030326020726
47493CB00004B/1175